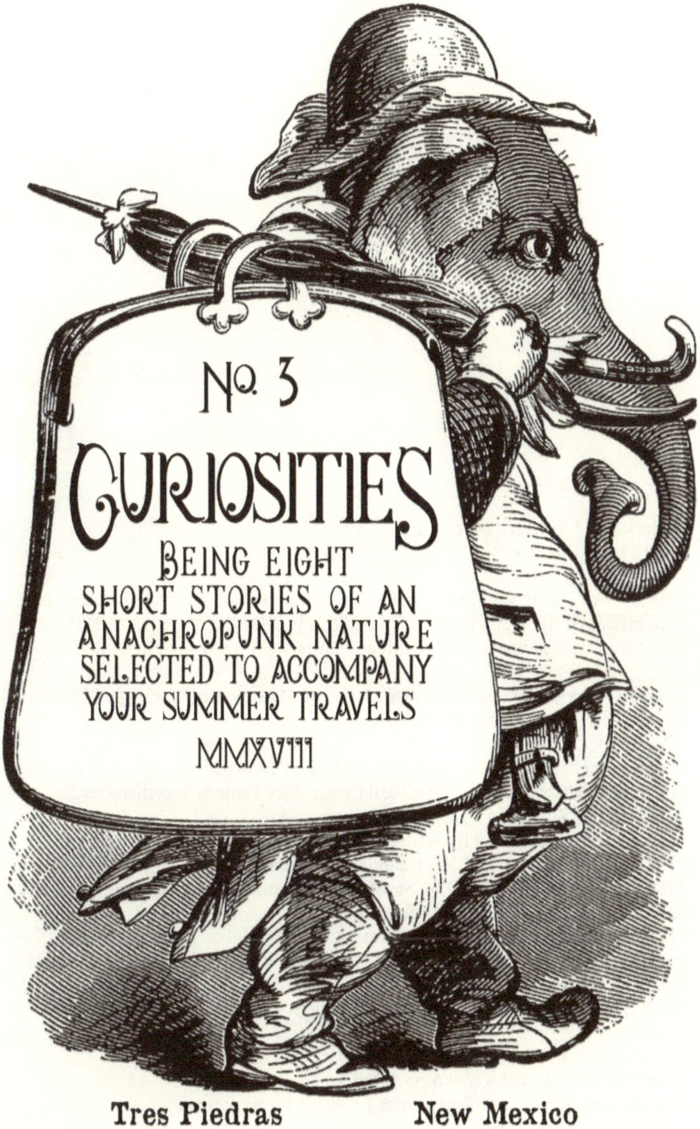

Nº 3

CURIOSITIES

BEING EIGHT
SHORT STORIES OF AN
ANACHROPUNK NATURE
SELECTED TO ACCOMPANY
YOUR SUMMER TRAVELS

MMXVIII

Tres Piedras   New Mexico

Curiosities #3 Summer 2018.
©2018 by Kevin Frost

Cover art: "Home for the Evening" ©2017 by Justin Tiang.
Title page clip art via Luminarium Graphics.
ToC clip art sourced from The British Library's Flickr albums.
Flatware clip art via The Old Design Shop.

ISBN-13: 978-1-948396-03-5 (Print on Demand)
ISBN-13: 978-1-948396-04-2 (EPUB)

Contents

Forewords: Road Trips, Podcasts, and Spring Submissions
Andrew McCurdy 3

The Rat and the Frog
Emma Whitehall 7

The Steam Elephant
Steven R. Southard 21

Doc Borden's Hard-Luck Hoss
Julie Frost 42

Gentlemanly Horrors of Mine Alone
Donald J. Bingle. 50

Kutsenko's Cage
William Burton McCormick 70

Waterproof
Marcelina Vizcarra. 90

The Traveler's Story of a Terribly Strange Bed
Wilkie Collins 96

Tea with Emma Whitehall
and Andrew McCurdy 114

Customer Service of the Priesthood of Thikra, Destroyer of Worlds and Creator of Light
Yasmine Fahmy 118

Contributors 122

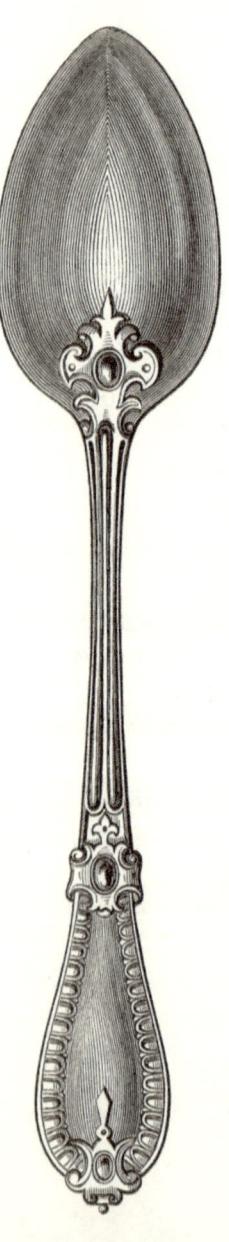

FOREWORDS: ROAD TRIPS, PODCASTS, AND SPRING SUBMISSIONS

July. Summer. The season of road trips, evening hikes, and deer flies. With more time in the car during the day, longer walks in the evening, and a nice set of headphones, I find I'm listening to podcasts and stories more than ever. As I write this, I reflect on what a marvelous future in which we live, a future in which cars, phones, and watches tell us stories.

When I was a kid, probably around my daughter's age of eleven, I had a little portable phonograph—the mid-seventies version of an iPod. Amongst my collection of big hair albums and period gems like "Nightflight to Venus" by Boney M (it featured a singing Cylon, how could anybody who ever heard it not love it?), was a substantial collection of stories in record form. My audible library had started a few years prior with Disney versions of classics, such as *Johnny Appleseed* and *The Headless Horseman.* Thurl Ravenscroft's voice in The Headless Horseman scared the hell out of me but it had countless more listens than Dennis Day's Johnny Appleseed. Over time the story collection became more eclectic. *Planet of the Apes, The Six Million Dollar Man,* and *Star Trek* were gradually overtaken by an ever-increasing selection of classics like *The Time Machine, 20,000 Leagues Under the Sea,* and *Frankenstein.*

I'm happy this issue of the Gallery continues to include vintage stories alongside new pieces This issue's vintage tale is "The Traveler's Story of a Terribly Strange Bed" by Wilkie Collins. The punctuation and paragraph formatting on this one has been abridged to suit modern tastes. This story first appeared in an 1852 edition of *Household Words,* a magazine edited by Charles Dickens.

The other tales that comprise this issue are taken from submissions to our podcast, some from the most recent round in June. The slush pile (as we affectionately refer to our electronic reading room) was filled to capacity with an abundance of fantastic adventures, weird tales, and strange trips. It was hard to keep up, fortunately, the quality of the stories was a motivating reinforcement. On a typical day, in the later part of the afternoon, I'd check the submission spreadsheet to see what new titles Kevin had added that day. At an unyielding pace, the pile grew.

The final tally for the June round was 264 submissions. Of those, we purchased eleven pieces. Eleven for 264 is just one of many stats I can tell you about. In his spare time, Kevin likes to play around in the spreadsheet. I think it's some sort of retired-math-teacher thing. It's great, though, because now I can click on 'Fun Facts' and see all kinds of neat trivia. For example, from the submissions that included monsters, the most popular monsters, based on number of appearances, in order, were: (1st) ghosts; (2nd) witches; (3-way-tie) zombie, fae, vampire. Less common, but all making at least a single appearance: a Wendigo, an Undine, a Selkie, a gargoyle, and various talking body parts that slipped over from the bizarro side of the house.

There are are four of us to sift the pit, with occasional guest reviewers eager (or conscripted) to join the party. If you are a regular listener of the podcast you may recognize the host making occasional reference to, or even chatting with, caricatures of ourselves, a group of less-than-willing writers-in-residence.

Those of us who comprise the Gallery reviewers, love what we do. I have read and discussed so many stories with the other reviewers over the past two years that within a paragraph, some-times within a sentence, and, on occasion by the title alone, I know which pieces will appeal to which reviewer. We comple-ment each other like a well drawn venn diagram. Kevin goes for old-school horror, Lovecraftian manic-terror, or body-gruesome chills. Jed likes the historical fictions and weird west submissions, with an eye towards the military, law enforcement and adventure. Steadman, with his Lit degree, is the only one amongst us with any style, and while he can sling mud as well as anyone, he still looks dapper at the end of the evening. Steadman likes the well-written, more literary submissions, with, perhaps, a dash of intelligent fantasy. Finally, I tend to be more partial to those submissions that are light and humourous, with extra points for the trippy or surprising.

I think the end result of our array of tastes and selection process is reflected well in the current collection. The variety of the story represents us well. We read all the submissions. It's a lot of work, but fortunately, Jed has a still. Her drinks are near toxic but they keep us energized.

I enjoy reading the stories as much as I enjoy listening to them on the Gallery podcast. And I must say, hearing them through my car, or phone, or watch, is a lot easier than carrying around that old portable record player.

Andrew McCurdy
Yarmouth, Nova Scotia
July 2018

"I think I can survive without a ladder, thank you," replied the Rat Prince.

THE RAT AND THE FROG
EMMA WHITEHALL

Lucinda Belmonte stood in the centre of a whirlwind of dresses. Silks and satins shimmered past her head as she flung the contents of her wardrobe behind her—while Ida tried to rescue the most expensive pieces from hitting the floor, where they risked being trampled upon by her mistress' house-shoes.

"I mean, really Ida—what *does* one wear to the launch of a *crypto*-menagerie? Is the blue silk too much? Not enough? Who *knows*!"

"I know, ma'am."

"I don't mean to sound un*grateful*, Ida, Lord knows *that*—but I just *wish* dear Devon had given me a little more context for the evening."

Yes. Dear Devon. Ida compressed a shudder at the mention of Lord Casterbury, Lucinda's paramour, into a single, slightly-longer-than-average blink. She'd already made a list of chores to be conveniently attending to when his automated carriage pulled up at the front door.

Lord Casterbury, in an attempt to impress his would-be betrothed, had invested a sizeable sum into a new wing at the Schuyler Museum of Crypto-Marine Biology, and had wrangled two tickets to the opening of the new Hippocamp exhibit. Unfortunately for him, Lucinda had about as much interest or experience with sea-life as his clockwork moustache-waxer. But, as Casterbury had informed her, the scientist who had captured the beasts was very fashionable–Malko something-or-other–and everyone worth seeing in Loxport would be in attendance. And so it was written in the pocket-diary, so shall it be done.

A sharp rap upon the front door. Lucinda squeaked.

"*Oh*! Ida, go show him into the parlour. I won't be a moment."

"...but ma'am, the dresses, and my sweeping..."

"You'll have time once we go, now *shoo*...and offer him a *nice* teacup, Ida–from the *special* set!"

Ida creaked the front door open as wide as she dared.

"Ah, the scrumptious Ida!"

"...Lord Casterbury."

Ida was a lot of things. 'Scrumptious' had never been one of them. 'Serious,' yes. 'Scrawny,' definitely. She jerked the corner of her mouth into a smile.

"Miss Belmonte won't be a moment. Please, take a seat in the drawing room, and I'll fetch you a cup of tea..."

"Only if you'll sit on my lap while I drink it," winked Casterbury. Ida blinked again, her smile frozen grimly onto her face.

"Devon, *darl*ing!"

Lucinda, arriving seconds too late, as usual. She'd plumped for the blue silk with a jaunty white fascinator–obviously going for a nautical theme. She drifted down the stairs–never betraying the feats of acrobatics she must have performed to pour herself into that dress without Ida's help–her hand already extended for a kiss.

"Lucinda, you look absolutely breathtaking. A mermaid, a siren, a rare ocean jewel..."

"Oh, Devon, *stop* it—you'll make me blush."

"If I could, I'd make you blush every hour, of every day, my angel."

Ida longed for her sweeping. She excused herself and retreated upstairs to begin the labour of organising Lucinda's dresses—with one ear pricked for the sound of the front door banging closed, and quiet finally returning to the household. She had her own agenda to keep tonight.

After she finished her chores, she completed a quick sweep of the house. Her job was always a simple one: one teacup to wash, floors that only needed a light mopping. And a mistress so spoiled and absent-minded, she had no real inkling of how long any given task should take. Which freed up a lot of Ida's evenings.

She climbed the ladder to her own quarters, fishing the old leather case from beneath her bed. She shed her maid's uniform, pulling on the black tunic and gent's trousers that fit like a second skin. The tight, black curls of her hair were slicked back with Macassar Oil, and her unusually wide feet slipped into a pair of steel-toed boots—fitted with foam to soften her step. She patted the pockets of her overcoat; yes, her lockpicks were there, where she'd left them. Finally, she held the goggles in her hand. Two bottle-green eyes stared back at her on a simple leather strap, their many dials supple and well-oiled. One small twist and Ida could see in any light condition. They were the most valuable thing she owned—her mother's—and she wouldn't trade them for all the gold in the world.

She allowed herself a moment of vanity, glancing in her scratched, dull full-length mirror. Gone was Ida, maid and confidant. In her place stood The Rat Prince.

The Rat Prince had evaded the constables for over three years now. Unlike Loxport's usual bevy of suspects, he was subtle, quick and clever: sneaking into the houses of the city's elite, stealing jewels, documents and, once, a pair of irreplaceable china dogs, before vanishing into the night—no windows broken, no fingerprints, no calling card. He was all at once working-class hero and monster of legend—a shadow on the wall.

Sometimes, Ida heard of some trinket on the grapevine and knew it would fetch a pretty penny, even after being bought and sold through a chain of middlemen and false identities—she'd even started a bidding war between two of her alter-egos, once. Sometimes she was just bored. But with most jobs—like tonight—a client had contacted her through one of her many channels and requested her services. Their meeting was scheduled for about five o'clock in the morning—an hour and a half before Ida's chores for the day usually started. Plenty of time.

She grabbed a new edition to her repertoire for the evening —a large, earthenware milk jug from the pantry—swung out of her bedroom window, and was up on the roof in one smooth motion. Ida let the cool air hit her face, breathing deep.

The city of Loxport unfolded before her like a strip of black satin, dotted with jewels. Genteel townhouses and parks dissolved into museums, theatres and exhibition halls, before fading into the pubs, terraces and docks down by the river. Ida charted her course, chin resting on her knuckles: over the rooftops, down the back alley near the University, round the back of the campus, up the drainpipe, two more roofs to jump, and she'd be there.

When Casterbury had arrived at the front door, brandishing two tickets to that damn soiree, Ida's stomach had sank. Her own plans had been scheduled in for months: as soon as Lucinda was asleep, she'd head off to the Schuyler, get the job done, and be back before she needed to start making breakfast.

Damn Casterbury. Ida had loathed him from the first instant he crossed her threshold, with his ruddy face, baying laugh and bristling, ticklish moustache. It was bad enough that, once he inevitably got his way and became a permanent resident, Ida would have to work twice as hard, and be twice as careful at covering up her night-time exploits. She can imagine her new lord and master becoming something of a snoop. But Ida would never understand why in God's name had her mistress picked someone so loud, so dull, so... *boorish.*

God—she'd been working for Lucinda for too long. She was starting to pick up her affects.

Ida shrugged herself out of her thoughts. She might have to move on sooner rather than later, but that was a thought for another time. She had to get going.

She stood, backed up, and took off at a run, taking the first of seventeen long leaps she'd plotted to get to the Schuyler. She landed neatly, lightly, and was off running again in her next stride, her heart pounding joyfully in her chest. God, she had missed this. Every day that was filled with nothing but sweeping and dusting was, in Ida's opinion, a wasted opportunity.

The Schuyler Museum was filled with couples wandering between the exhibits—tanks filled with flitting fish of every colour, first editions of famous texts, and skeletons of imposing beasts such as the Kraken, the Ammochostos and the giant whales. Waiters, bottles in hand, floated from group to group, filling glasses with shimmering wine. One wall of the most populated room was taken up with a huge tank, filled with miniature, horse-like creatures that sped through the water, challenging the guests through the glass and playing in the seaweed of their new habitat. Beside them stood their captor: Doctor Odessa Malko, a tall, ramrod-straight woman, blonde hair tied back in a plait, politely smiling at guests as, one by one, they approached her to congratulate her on the new exhibit. Everyone's attention was fixed on the Doctor, or the exhibits, or each other. Not one person noticed a shadow flick across the room from above.

Ida, perched on the catwalk above, and got her bearings. This wasn't her first time in the Schuyler Museum—three of the museum's most treasured trinkets had made their way out the building in her pockets. Her route into and through the building was as well-plotted as the optimal way to mop Lucinda's pantry.

Her target wasn't in this room, obviously—far too risky, even for The Rat Prince. No, she was looking to find The Henrietta Wing.

"The exhibit isn't technically open to the public yet," her

client had said. "They stagger these things, and it gives the exhibit a chance to...acclimatise. You shouldn't have too much trouble getting to the wing itself, and there will be a ladder behind the door to assist you once you're in."

"I think I can survive without a ladder, thank you," replied The Rat Prince from the shadows, green eyes glinting in the low lamplight. "If you have people on the inside, why do you need me?"

"None of us have the skills you possess. Will you help us, or no?"

"Well," the Rat Prince snickered, "I've always been known as a kind-hearted soul. Just have the money ready when I get there."

Ida followed the catwalk, her eye trained on every door, every sign. The Malko Wing, where most of the guests were still milling. Then the Hightower Wing, the Tilikum, the Cowperthwaite...

Aha.

The Henrietta Wing—named for Henrietta von Haler, Director of the Schuyler Museum, Ida was informed by the bronze plaque on the wall—featured a large, blocky archway, with a pair of dark oak doors. A circular locking mechanism, around the size of Ida's fist, hung from the handles of the door by a large metal chain. A gear at each "corner" of the circle rotated four small discs in the middle of the device—when they were in the correct position, the door would open. Ida fished her lockpick kit from her overcoat. Holding a narrow, hooked hex key in one hand, she gently began teasing the gears into place, feeling for the moments when the metal felt the most worn. Behind her, she could hear the sounds of guests laughing, glasses clinking and subtle music playing. Then:

"Is it not my break yet?"

"C'mon, Tom—you've only been here two hours."

"I know, but watching them waiters running about with that blackberry wine..."

"No drinking on the job, I've told you already. C'mon, let's do another patrol, then I might let you go on a break."

Ida's hand slipped—damnit, now she'd have to start this dial again. Her heart beat faster in her chest: not afraid, not yet, but full of the knowledge she'd have to pick up her pace.

The footsteps grew louder. As the guards bickered about their shifts and the quality of blackberry wine, Ida felt the gear slide into place. As the shadows of the guards grew on the wall, she slipped inside and pulled the door to behind her.

The Henrietta Wing was pitch-black and cool. Ida spun a dial on her goggles, and the details of the room slowly came into green-tinged view. Three of the walls were bare, with the back one engineered to look like a ruddy coastline; plaster rocks and jagged, painted clifftops. In the centre sat a cylindrical tank. The water inside was a strange grey colour, still and cold-looking. Ida approached it, fishing the jug from her bag. Her prize was in there. All that remained was to acquire it.

Sure enough, a wooden ladder leaned against the right-hand wall. Ida snorted. Ladder, indeed. She jammed the toe of one boot into a crevice in the façade and began her climb.

About two-thirds of the way up, Ida maneuvered herself to face the tank, hands gripping the plaster behind her. She stared into the water, searching for this creature she'd been sent to kidnap.

Out of the murk came what Ida could only describe as a frog. A grey-green frog, nearly as long as Ida's forearm, with big bulging eyes and webbed fingers and huge gills. *I'm sure I caught one of those in the River Lox when I was a kid*, Ida thought. Still, money is money. She reached for the lid of the tank, attempted what she hoped was a reassuring smile.

"Hello...little fellow. I've come to take you—"

The creature unhinged its jaw and screeched, the sound reverberating through the glass, distorted and strange. Its maw stretched impossibly wide, and impossibly black. Rows upon rows of fine, dagger-sharp teeth spiralled down its throat. Ida started, her grip slipping and her ears ringing. She fell with a thud to the floor, her teeth clamping down mercilessly on her tongue.

"Ow! Damnit—"

The door opened.

"Oh, Devon—you're *sure* we won't get caught?"

"Nonsense, darling—the door was unlocked, so it's obviously permitted. Besides, what am I putting my pounds and pence towards, if not a private viewing for my ocean jewel?"

Ida slumped back against the façade, her knees against her chest, praying she'd be mistaken for a boulder through the dirty glass. This couldn't be happening. No, she couldn't be this unlucky. She'd hit her head, that was it, and now she was hallucinating...

No. There was Lucinda's silhouette through the glass. And there was bloody goddamn Devon pissing Casterbury's fat form, gesturing and pontificating about. Ida would have almost preferred the guards.

"...brought it back from some expedition to the Americas. Some tiny coastal town...Inns-something. Got caught in a net, poor devil, and the townsfolk sold it to us. It won't be going on display for, oh a few more months yet—"

"It's a frog."

"...What was that?"

"It's a *frog*, Devon. A big, slimy frog—ugh, how *awf*ul! I much preferred those *pretty* little fish, or the *sweet* little Hippopotomuses—"

"Hippocamps, darling—"

Ida heard the unmistakable clack of Lucinda stamping her tiny feet.

"I demand to be taken back to the party, *now.*"

Yes, Lucinda, Ida thought. *Back to the party. Back to the music and the pretty fish and the blackberry wine, go on now...*

Casterbury's voice took on a lecherous slink. "Oh, Lucinda darling—I didn't bring you in here just for the exhibit. I have been simply dying to get you alone all evening. You look so ravishing, you can barely blame me for that..."

A giggle. Ida's heart sank, lost in her churning stomach.

"I suppose there is a *hint* of *r*omance to sneaking *off* like this..."

"A darkened room, the risk of discovery..."

"Oh *Devon...*"

And so, over the next twelve minutes, Ida Finn silently descended into the depths of her own personal hell.

Finally–*finally!*–the giggles and hushed conversation from the other side of the tank faded away, and the door to the Henrietta Wing softly closed again, and Ida was again alone. She scurried back up the façade, and peered into the darkness of the water below her. The fog-thing was floating, suspended, about two feet into the water, motionless.

"Are you as traumatised as I am at that display?" Ida muttered. "As least you're getting out. That's my life, matey."

She spent a moment or two trying to coax the creature to her. Ida didn't have a lot of experience with animals–one of her past employees had had a Pug, but Ida and Countess Mitzie had not been bosom chums. She tried making that squeaky noise with her lips that animal lovers made to call their pets to them–no joy. She tapped the water gently, cooing "c'mon, c'mon" The creature glanced up at her, then resumed its motionless suspension. There was nothing else for it. Groaning under her breath, Ida plunged her right hand into the water up to the elbow, shoving the frog-thing by its undercarriage into the jug. It squawked and tried to turn to snap at her, webbed hands clawing at the surface of the water. Ida slammed the lid of the jug closed, one hand clamping it shut, the other clutching it to her chest as she wrenched it out of the water.

Alright. The easy part was over.

Ida slid as carefully as she could back down the façade, and made her way towards the door. Outside, the party was still in full swing. If she could get back up into the rafters, she'd be home safe...

Lucinda's laugh, pretty and shrill as a songbird, rang out from just beyond the door. Ida had counted on her mistress staying at the hub of the evening's festivities. Now, thanks to *Dear Devon,* she was a loose cannon. Ida saw her carefully planned, reliable route up and out of the Schuyler Museum crumble before her eyes.

Pushing the air from her lungs in a long, steady sigh, Ida considered her options. Hide in the façade and wait until the party ended? No—her client was expecting her. Throw the doors open and strut through the party, knocking back some wine on her way out the front doors? Tempting, but the constables would be waiting for her before she'd emptied her glass.

The creature kicked miserably at the walls of the jug. Ida empathised. Her hand idled at the strap of her goggles, turning the dials absently as her mind searched for a solution—a bad habit of hers. If she couldn't find a solution with one exposure, she would open and close the aperture on her goggles—as if a new brightness or darkness would bring a new perspective on her thoughts. When she was a child, her mother had slapped her hands away so often that both their palms stung.

"You'll break them, Ida."

"Sorry, Mum—"

" 'Mama'—I've told you enough times to call me 'Mama', haven't I? 'Mum' is common. I'll not have you being outed as a gutterbrat on your first day in some Lord's house."

Ida, seven years old, felt tears burn at her eyelashes. Her mother's face loomed before her, her worn brown hands cupping Ida's cheeks. Her face was filled with a stubborn, fierce kind of love.

"It's for your own good, sweetheart. No daughter of mine is going to grow up in poverty. Now, I've hidden your dolly some-where in the house. Why don't you try and find it? You can have a sugared almond if you do."

Suddenly, back in the real world, a flash of light snagged on the corner of Ida's field of vision. She looked up—there, above her, was a tiny rectangular window, up by the domed ceiling. It was small—purely to ventilate the room without destroying the delicate ambience—but a scoundrel as skinny as The Rat Prince could surely fit through it.

Ida considered the façade. The creature lurched from side to side in the jug. She couldn't navigate the rocks one-handed without risking the damned thing launching itself out the jug and down to its death. She needed something secure, something easy to navigate, something like a...

Damnit.

Ida walked towards the ladder with bitter resignation. Hooking the jug under one arm, she began her ascent.

Ida was correct: a skinny scoundrel like The Rat Prince could fit through the tiny rectangular window. A skinny scoundrel carrying a milk jug containing a squirming frog-thing, however, could not. The jug clanked and banged against the window-frame as Ida attempted to maneuver it out onto the roof of the Schuyler Museum. The frog-thing belched and squawked its displeasure.

"Come on, you stupid thing," Ida muttered. "I'm trying to save your damn –"

"What's going on up there?"

As Ida looked down and saw the constable far below her on the pavement, a crowd of passers-by stopping to look in the direction of his pointing finger, three things happened at once. The first was that her grip on the jug loosened, just for a fraction of a moment. The next was that the lid of the jug flew open, and the frog-thing, free at last, leapt out onto the roof beside her with a wet-sounded thud. The third was that Ida decided that this was the worst job she had ever taken on.

"It's The bloody Rat Prince!"

"What's that you say, Sir?"

"The Rat Prince! He's–"

"There, up there! He's–"

"–stolen something from the Schuyler!"

"What is that thing?"

"Halt, in the name of the law!"

The constable had dashed inside the building, and the frog-thing had begun its slow, ponderous hop towards the edge of the rooftop. As it looked down, the creature let out another of those horrific screams–uninhibited this time by the thick glass of its tank. The sound was all-encompassing, and as Ida leapt, tucking her body into a forward roll, she caught a glimpse of the crowd below crumple to the ground, clutching at their ears. Ida scooped the creature up as she tumbled over it. Carrying it under her arm like a bundle of laundry, she took a running leap off the side of the Schuyler Museum. Her breath felt like fire in her throat, and the creature finally got its nasty little teeth into her skin. Ida bit back the pain, resisting the urge to chuck the little beast down to the crowd below and make a run for it. Instead, she slid down drainpipes and scurried up trellises, sliding over the rooftops of houses and universities, darting like a hunted fox over Loxport until the baying echoes of her name—imagined or otherwise—no longer rang in her ears. Only then did she make her way towards the docks.

Her client was leaning against a lamp-post, his hooded robe covering his face.

"You're twenty-three minutes late," he murmured, as The Rat Prince slipped out from behind a dingy-looking public house.

"Yes, well," snarled The Rat Prince, rubbing pointedly at the bite marks on his arm, "you'd be late too if you'd had the night I have. Here's your monster, safe and well."

The client held out his arms, and the frog-thing leapt into his embrace, snuggling into the crook of his neck like a kitten. Beneath his goggles, The Rat Prince scowled.

"Ny'anthys blesses you for the safe return of her child," the client said, his smile flashing in the shadows of his hood.

"Fantastic. Does Ny'anthys have my money?"

Unhearing, the client knelt at the edge of the dock, guiding the frog-thing back into the water. It slipped below the surface, and for a moment, everything was quiet. Then the client began chanting something under his breath—low and fast and not in any language that Ida had ever heard. The water in the Loxport docks began to froth and boil, and a huge, humped back rose from within it—the back of a creature that was far too large for even the deepest waters of the dock to be a comfortable fit. This creature—if it could be called something as mundane as a creature—was from a place so dark, and so deep, that it was beyond the comprehension of even those most intelligent scientists that had danced and drank inside the Schuyler that night. The idea of the two species inhabiting the same plane of existence, let alone the same building, was laughable to the point of hysteria.

Two gigantic, bulbous eyes looked back at the humans on the dock's edge, and both of them felt their sanity shift, just for a moment, out of their grasp. The world spiralled and tipped to one side. Then, the small frog-creature resurfaced, darting through the froth as happily as a dolphin. The massive creature's gaze softened, and one huge, webbed hand scooped up its baby. The eldritch mother and child returned to the open ocean with one last gigantic flume of water.

The waves lapped at the sides of the dock. Somewhere, far in the distance, seagulls returned to their roosts on the riggings of the boats that had survived the small tsunami. The Rat Prince turned, hand outstretched.

"Well. That was strange. Money now, please."

◎   ◎   ◎

"...really was a *won*derful night, Ida darling, I *wish* you'd been there..."

"Me too, ma'am. It sounds wonderful."

"It's just such a *shame* about those *poor* people. Terrorised by that *aw*ful *Rat Prince*!"

"I know, ma'am."

"I read in the paper that he's got some sort of *weap*on now—some sort of *sonic* what-have-you, Devon says, that he used to *decompasitate* that poor constable, so he could make his escape!"

"Sounds ghastly, ma'am—would you like Apricot or Plum jam this morning?"

"*Plum*, darling. Just *promi*se me you'll be careful on your errands, or when you're alone in your quarters at night...if anything happened to you..."

Lucinda's eyes glittered with emotion. Ida patted her mistress' hand.

"I promise, ma'am."

Lucinda's fingers brushed against the bandage that snaked

up her maid's arm, and her eyes narrowed as she caught Ida wince.

"Heavens, Ida—what have you done to your arm?"

Ida rubbed at the bandage, embarrassed.

"Cat-scratches, ma'am. I tried to befriend that little black tomcat that we see in the garden from time to time..."

A beat. Then, Lucinda rolled her eyes.

"I never had you down as an *animal* lover, Ida! *Hon*estly, befriending *strays*. You're too kind-hearted for your own good!"

"That's me, ma'am."

"*Now*, go on, up to your quarters. I'll call on you when I desire my bath to be run."

As Ida climbed the steps to her room, she felt the aches and pains of the previous night flood back into her muscles. Unwatched by her mistress, she let herself slouch, and she fell into bed as heavily as a stone. She was exhausted, her ears still rang from the shrieks of that horrid little monster she'd nearly got herself arrested trying to save, and she'd suffered throughout the night with nightmares of frothing waves, gigantic beasts with bulbous eyes, and gigantic, impossible kingdoms far below the waves...

Still, she thought, popping a freshly sugared almond into her mouth from the bag she stashed below her pillow, *the job still had some perks. Just no more rescue missions from now on, perhaps...*

THE STEAM ELEPHANT

STEVEN R. SOUTHARD

"By Jove, we've been called up!" Colonel Edward Munro's bearded jowls shook as he summed up the missive he held.

"Called up? To where? Why?" I broke the silence when no one else did.

"It's war, man. Against the wretched Zulus. Frere gave them every opportunity, but it appears they've rebuffed him. According to this, Commissioner Frere is willing to pay us to assist the Army."

Captain Hood frowned and asked, "Can't they bloody well wait until our hunt's over?"

Sir Edward Munro, now fifty-nine years old, looked each of us in the eye as if able to weigh our thoughts before making up his mind. His gaze passed over the servants, then me, Banks, and Hood before lingering on his wife, Laura. He looked back at the uniformed courier who'd brought the war news, and whose horse still panted from the ride. The Colonel, I thought, would turn down this request. He'd endured his share of battles and deserved a peaceful retirement after the events in India a decade ago.

Sir Edward folded and pocketed the communiqué. "You may tell the High Commissioner," Munro straightened to full height and his eyes blazed with a fierceness I'd not seen for years, "that as long as England needs me, I shall never let her down. Further, I shall accept not one pound in payment."

With a "Very good, sir," the messenger snapped a salute and rode off to the northeast.

"I suppose I can bring down Zulus as well as lions," Hood muttered, examining his rifle as if looking for some adjustment to make for his new prey.

"Darling," the Colonel turned to Lady Munro. "We shall let you off at Durban where you can catch the next supply ship to London."

"No," Laura spoke with a firm determination honed by a life as hard as her husband's. "We suffered a separation of nine years, and I'll not part from you again. Besides," she smiled at him, "where else would I be as safe?"

"Stubborn woman," Munro shook his head and rolled his eyes. "Now as for you, Monsieur Maucler," he turned to me. "This isn't your fight. Strictly a British affair, you know. I'll arrange for your transport back to Paris."

"My friends," I found myself saying, "how can I abandon you, after all we've been through together?"

◎　◎　◎

So we ended our search for leonine prey and began our journey out of Natal toward Zululand.

We traveled, as we'd done in India, by steam elephant.

Munro had commissioned Banks to design and build a massive iron elephant, its ponderous jointed legs driven by a powerful traction steam engine. The driver steered its course from a howdah mounted on its back. Smoke from its boiler belched from its upturned trunk. At night, gas lanterns beamed light from the animal's eyes. Curved, scythe-like metal tusks jutted from the mouth area. The mighty animal towed two wheeled carriages behind it, each equipped with comfortable living quarters and spacious verandas. Years earlier, Banks had built a similar construction for the Rajah of Bhootan, modeling it after the Indian species of elephant. We'd had numerous adventures in India while in the company of that beast—named Behemoth—prior to its destruction, all described somewhat over-dramatically by Monsieur Jules Verne in his *Steam House* accounts. Improving on our faithful old Behemoth, Banks had patterned his new elephant after the African species. We'd named this one Mastodon, and called the entire arrangement—Mastodon and his two carriages—our Steam House.

For the past three months, we enjoyed a safari while being towed by Mastodon across the southern parts of Africa. Staying for the most part in British colonies, we'd pursued lions and other game across the wilds of Transvaal, Cape Colony, and Natal. So far we had avoided Zululand due to the bloodthirsty reputation of its natives. All of us, and especially Captain Hood, had achieved success and we always provided our cook with sufficient meat to prepare for our meals. Then the messenger had found us and we'd accepted our new mission.

The elderly Scotsman, Colonel Edward Munro, formerly commander of the 93rd Regiment of Highlanders during the Sepoy uprising in India, led our party. Laura, his wife, thought to have died at a massacre in Cawnpore, driven insane by the horrors she'd seen there, had wandered alone across the Indian countryside for many years. Reunited with her husband, she'd since made a complete recovery and refused to leave his side. Auburn-haired Captain Hood, once with the first squadron of Carabineers, and an avid huntsman, also traveled with our band. Banks, a talented railway engineer, accompanied us as well. Seven attendants of various nationalities and skills rounded out our group. This number included servants, a cook, and an African guide.

Mastodon trod at a steady pace of fifteen miles per hour over the Natal landscape. The metal pachyderm rumbled along, each cylindrical foot lifting, advancing, and lowering in turn through a cycle designed to smooth the ride as much as possible. Even so, the howdah swayed some during the four-legged gait. For those of us being towed behind, the carriage wheels leveled our ride, and we got used to a measure of jerkiness in our forward motion.

I marveled at how the driver within his howdah, and the engineman and stoker within the beast's belly, could bear the combined heat of the African summer and a steam boiler without a word of complaint.

We kept to the savannas, skirting the edge of forests and jungles, avoiding steep hills. Crossing the occasional shallow river presented no obstacle to us, for Banks had constructed the elephant and both carriages to be waterproof and able to float. I found it amusing how, with the engine secured, Banks could cause Mastodon's trunk to rotate down and into these rivers, and draw water up into storage tanks for the boilers.

To Captain Hood's extreme frustration, the countryside teemed with lions now that our hunt had ended. He begged the Colonel for a slight respite from our march so he could take down some of these felines, but Munro refused.

During the hunt, we had been stopping at night while the servants gathered wood fuel, allowing Banks and his engineman to conduct maintenance. Now headed for war, we kept going at all hours, Mastodon's lantern eyes blazing forth to guide our way after dark.

"Colonel, I think we need to prepare Mastodon for battle," Banks said on the day after our redirection.

"What do you mean, Banks?"

"You see, I designed it for hunting game that doesn't shoot back. I think I should shield the howdah and the carriages against spears and rifle shots."

"How would you do that?"

"Pietermaritzburg is not far ahead. There's a forge and a foundry there. Give me a few days and I can armor these carriages and convert Mastodon into a proper war elephant."

"War elephant," Colonel Munro puffed his pipe. "Rather

like the sound of that. I'll be a modern-day Hannibal. Over the Alps to take on the Roman legions!" He laughed. "Of course, these Zulus warlords aren't exactly centurions. Very good, Banks, dress up Mastodon for battle."

A week later, we departed northward from Pietermaritzburg with riveted iron plating covering all exposed parts of the howdah and both carriages. From inside, we could cover and uncover various rectangular slits for viewing and shooting. I feared that the steam engine would prove insufficient for pulling that additional weight, but Mastodon marched right along at his usual pace.

On 11 January, 1879, we joined up with the British Third Column. Camping for the night just outside Oskarberg, we greeted the men who wandered over to marvel at our conveyance. They wore scarlet jackets with diagonal white cordons, white helmets, ammunition belts, blue trousers, and black boots. Despite their long march that day, they looked confident, eager for battle.

In accordance with protocol, Colonel Munro called on the commander of this column, Lieutenant-General Frederic Thesiger, known as the Baron Lord Chelmsford, and invited this personage to tour our Steam House. Lord Chelmsford, along with his second, accepted and later settled into the drawing room of our first carriage for drinks and a smoke.

"Glad you're here, Munro," Chelmsford said. A tall man, with hair parted just to the left of center and a thick black beard, he impressed me as being a proper Victorian gentleman. "I've had a beastly time dragging my army over these plains. The oxen and mules can haul our supply wagons only ten miles a day. They must rest and graze for most of the day or they expire. Why, your elephant could likely pull two wagons by itself, a job I now use thirty oxen to do, and yours has no need of rest."

"Mastodon is more than just a substitute ox, my Lord," Munro replied. "He's a proper war elephant. With him, we'll triumph over these Zulus in short order."

Lord Chelmsford waved his pipe with a dismissive air.

"Don't worry about the natives. In fact, I may have to draw them out to get them to fight at all. No, my problem is logistical, the army traveling on its stomach, that sort of thing."

Munro seemed about to become more defensive about his elephant, but I changed the subject to what I thought would be a safer topic. "Lord Chelmsford, if I may, since news has been sporadic in this region, can you enlighten us about the cause of this war?"

Only the crickets outside filled the five-second silence that followed my faux pas.

"Maucler's French," Munro explained, "and a good friend."

Only that latter fact, I speculated, kept me from being dismissed on the spot.

"Well, *Monsieur Maucler,*" Chelmsford enunciated each syllable as if clarifying for a slow child, "in the British Army, we are accustomed to following orders, not questioning them. My orders are to defeat the Zulu forces or bring them to the point of surrender. I have little time or inclination to speculate on the politics of this affair."

"Yes, you'll have the rest of your life to wonder about politicians who don't dirty themselves with fighting," Colonel Munro mused, no doubt reflecting on his experiences in India. To my relief he added, "Actually sir, I quite agree with Maucler on this point. It's good for the lads to know why they're risking their lives fighting on foreign soil. Not questioning orders, you see, but understanding their context."

Lord Chelmsford regarded the older man for a time. Though far outranking the retired Colonel, he nonetheless had to respect Munro's experience. "I do know this much. Sir Henry Frere, the High Commissioner for South Africa, issued a direct ultimatum. The corrupt Zulu warlord ignored it, simple as that. Thus, the belligerent, bloodthirsty bastards have driven us to war." He puffed his pipe.

"My Lord," Captain Hood spoke up, "what's your plan for hunting down and defeating these Zulus?"

"I'd like nothing more than to march east sixty-five miles to

Ulundi, the capital. But first, we must subdue a Zulu stronghold north of here. Can't very well afford to leave them able to attack us from behind." He regarded Colonel Munro. "Can we count on you, tomorrow—"

"With pleasure, sir," Munro beamed.

"—to transport some troops and ammo to the site?"

◎   ◎   ◎

We set out early the next day for the stronghold. Officers, including Lord Chelmsford, rode horseback alongside. Forty soldiers and several crates of ammunition accompanied us, evenly split within the two carriages. Mastodon did not slow his speed despite the additional load.

On the way, I stole a moment of Colonel Munro's time to speak in private. "I'm sorry if I insulted his Lordship last night. I assure you—"

"Don't worry about it, Maucler. For a Lieutenant General, the man completely lacks strategic vision. He's like one of the blind men in that old parable. When in the presence of our elephant, he declares it to be an ox!"

Moving north along the east bank of the Bashee River, we came upon a *spruit,* feeding the river from highlands to the east. We turned in that direction, and in a few miles, grassland gave way to bare, rocky terrain. Ahead, the stream's banks angled upward into substantial hills. Unable to negotiate the incline, Mastodon therefore entered the flat-bottomed spruit and marched through the water into the narrow gorge.

Native herders tended cattle, goats, and sheep that grazed on the few tufts of grass remaining in this rocky ravine. Seeing the advance of our massive mechanical elephant belching smoke, they panicked and ran alongside their livestock farther into the gorge, yelling and waving their arms.

Gunfire erupted up ahead. From concealed places behind boulders and in the hill's caves and crevices, the Zulus were firing at us.

"They have rifles!" I couldn't have been more astonished.

"Enfields," Hood scoffed, squinting through the sights of his Martini-Henry. He fired, and one Zulu warrior dropped his weapon and slid down the hillside.

Our troops hurried out of the carriages and formed up into rows at the officers' command. Those of us in Munro's party remained on our carriage's forward veranda.

The fusillade from the hills quieted down, and a male voice sounded and echoed through the valley. In rough English, it asked, "By whose orders do you come here?"

One of the British officers yelled back, "By orders of the Great White Queen!"

This answer must not have pleased the natives, for they renewed firing, and began hurling spears and rolling boulders down toward us.

The officers gave the order to advance, and the men began scaling the hills, shooting as they went.

My trusty Chassepot carbine did more annoying than killing, I'm ashamed to say. Still, the Zulu's aim proved even worse, and only a couple of bullets glanced off Mastodon's steel hide.

Our driver gave a blast from the steam whistle, a sound reminiscent of an elephant's trumpeting. As one, the Zulu warriors rose from their hiding places and retreated farther into the ravine, moving with agility and speed over the steep, rocky surfaces. Somehow they gave the impression of a planned relocation rather than fearful scattering.

For the first time I could see our foe. Wearing simple loincloths, feathered headbands, and flowing white leggings, each man carried a thin oval shield and a short spear. All these accouterments matched in color and design.

After the Zulus vanished, our troops captured their livestock and set fire to their kraal, a collection of rude huts tucked well into the gorge. I witnessed one of our soldiers bayoneting wounded Zulus until ordered to stop by an officer. A total of twenty enemy warriors lay dead, while our forces suffered three wounded.

◉　◉　◉

Back at camp that evening everyone celebrated the victory. Brandy flowed in great quantities, hurrahs resounded through the camp, and Colonel Munro predicted a rapid end to the war.

Nagging worries kept me from sharing in the jubilation. I slipped out of the carriage and stood admiring our Mastodon, seeming to stand watch for us with his lantern eyes blazing, as if watching for a surprise Zulu night attack. The technicians made adjustments to the traction engine and provisioned the elephant with wood fuel and water.

"He did us right proud today, eh?" Banks, the engineer, appeared at my side, admiring his metal creation. He reached up and patted Mastodon's gray flanks. Banks swayed on his feet and slurred his words.

"Yes, indeed he did."

"You know, Maucler, I fancy we're looking at the future of land warfare here."

"What do you mean?"

"Can't you see it, man? Ten, twenty, a hundred Mastodons tromping across the battlefield, guns firing. Why, I could make the howdah rotate like an ironclad turret, and even mount cannon inside it. Aye, nothing could stand it his way. Mark my words, Mastodon will replace both foot soldiers and cavalry someday."

My mind's eye foresaw a different vision. What one nation could develop, others would soon copy. I saw Banks' battlefields too, but in my imagination, each army possessed its own steam-powered beasts. The ground trembled with their mighty footfalls; smoke from their trunks stung one's eyes; the cannons deafened. Some elephants lay toppled, reduced to burning hulks, all occupants dead. I shook my head to clear this nightmarish image and braved a smile. "Banks, you're the very engineer who could make that dream happen."

During the next few days, we stayed with Lord Chelmsford's center column forces as they slogged through marshes and over rocky foothills amidst driving rain. The trek gave me time to ponder the events of the skirmish at the gorge. The Zulu warriors had stood their ground for some time against the power of our sophisticated weaponry. From what I could see as they scampered over the rocks, they looked to be in better physical condition than our own troops. Even in retreat, they acted with admirable discipline and coordination.

We made temporary camp against the eastern slope of a mountain known as Isandlwana. It made an ideal location for a defensive camp—a ready supply of wood from *msasa* trees on the mountainside to our back, excellent visibility across the valley all the way to an escarpment rising up to Nquthu Plateau in the distance, and available water from a spruit running in a deep *donga,* or run-off ditch. As a precaution, Lord Chelmsford stationed mounted cavalry vedettes as scouts along the distant ridge to report any sightings of the Zulu army.

Days passed while troops came and went. Chelmsford dispatched Mastodon on occasional day trips to tow bogged-down wagons to camp. "Blasted ox duty," Munro grumbled.

On the 22nd, we awoke to the news that Lord Chelmsford had departed with six companies and a mounted infantry detachment during the night, in response to a report of an encounter with 1000 Zulus a few miles away. He left Lieutenant-Colonel Henry Pulleine in charge of the camp.

At about eight o'clock, a bugler sounded the 'fall in' signal and all the men took their defensive posts.

"A vedette says the whole bloody Zulu army is marching from the north-east towards us," said a nearby soldier. "Pass it on."

Thus did word spread throughout the camp. Within Mastodon and the carriages, we readied our rifles and ammunition, then sat on the veranda to scan the horizon.

An hour later, an entire column of British troops entered the camp.

"Those three battalions belong to Brevet-Colonel Durnford," relayed our word-of-mouth network. "He's a man of action, he is."

While we waited, distant rifle- and cannon-fire sounded at intervals. Vedettes rode in, made their reports at the command tent, and rode off.

"Durnford and Pulleine are arguing about who's in charge," said the camp gossip. "Durnford is senior, but doesn't have clear orders from Chelmsford. Ol' Durnford wants to take us all and go on the attack. Pulleine says we're to defend the camp. In other words, *Pulleine* won't *pull out!*" Our information source found his own joke far funnier than I did.

"Blast it all, this waiting has gone on long enough!" Munro thundered. He sent his servant, a Gurkha named Goûmi, to the command tent with a proposal.

Goûmi soon returned. "Sir, Colonel Pulleine orders us to remain here to guard the camp."

"Guard it?" Munro sputtered. "From whom? The Zulus are miles away, and other units are enjoying all the action!"

Goûmi had no answer, of course. We continued to wait. Durnford's forces marched out, heading northeast.

While eating lunch some time later, we began hearing a rhythmic pounding noise, soft but growing louder, like the far-off marching of a thousand booted soldiers. We sprang from the table and, from the veranda, saw an unending line of Zulu warriors standing on the distant plateau. The beating, thumping noise continued, interspersed with odd chants.

"Rapping their spears against their shields," observed Captain Hood, while I marveled at his eyesight. "Apparently, gentlemen, we are supposed to be scared."

The Zulu tide poured down into the valley. At least five separate groups converged toward our camp in a continuous arc from northeast to northwest. Five or ten thousand of them, it seemed, opposing the 1700 of us in the camp. Some groups ran at full speed clutching their shields and spears, while others marched, and still other groups hung back. A coordinated, pre-arranged attack.

"Men, our moment has arrived at last," Colonel Munro rose from his seat. "Man your posts! We fight for England!"

With the right side of Mastodon and his carriages facing the mountain, we each occupied rooms on the left side—Banks in the drawing room, Captain Hood in the dining room, Munro and I each in our own cabins. Goûmi and the other servants defended the second carriage. I raised one of the rectangular slits and peered out.

In the foreground of my view, a British platoon fired on command in ranks at the advancing Zulus. The first rank fired, and then knelt to reload while the second rank standing behind fired. Zulu warriors dropped with each volley, their shields having been designed to deflect spears, not bullets. A few of the Zulus fired rifles of their own, but struck no targets.

A 'seven pounder,' sounded off to my left. Landing amidst a tight company of Zulu fighters, the cannon's projectile mowed down a row of them in an instant.

Poking my rifle barrel through the slit, I took aim and shot at a group of warriors making a rush for the rifle platoon. Several dropped dead at once, due to massed fire from the platoon and from those of us within the Steam House. The remaining Zulus fell back and regrouped. They seemed to melt away, finding concealment behind clumps of vegetation or depressions in the ground. Looking beyond them, I could still see many thousands standing, waiting just beyond effective rifle range. *Testing us,* I thought, *probing our defenses for weak points.* I revised my estimate of their numbers upward to the range of twenty thousand. Out of my zone of vision to the right, I heard gunfire and shouts indicating a skirmish in that direction.

A mounted messenger rode up to our carriage and shouted, "Colonel Munro, sir!"

"Here, lad," the Colonel said.

From my room next to Munro's, I could hear every word of their conversation.

"Sir, Colonel Pulliene requests that you move a half mile that way—"

I couldn't see which way he pointed.

"—and support Colonel Durnford. His men are pinned down, low on ammunition. This morning, Colonel Pulliene promised him help if he needed it."

"Tell the Colonel we'll make good on his promise."

Munro shouted orders. "Banks! Get up steam! Sound the whistle! Time for our war elephant to march into the fray."

The servants hurried to their posts while the rest of us gathered in the drawing room.

"Sir," Banks touched Munro on the shoulder. "I'd like to drive Mastodon myself into battle today."

The engine-driver, Storr, had always guided Mastodon, and Behemoth before that.

"Highly irregular," Munro looked his friend in the eye. "But I can't refuse Mastodon's creator. Go, Banks."

Odd, I thought, for a gentleman to volunteer to perform the work of a common laborer. Whatever Banks' reasons, the Colonel respected them.

The Steam House began picking up speed. Amid loud clanking, hissing, and thudding we advanced with a speed I estimated as twenty-five miles per hour, Mastodon's trunk belching thick, black clouds of smoke.

Soon we reached the area of Durnford's besieged men. From what I could see, a tightening circle of natives surrounded the dwindling British troops. The Zulus fought with unmatched ferocity. With ammunition near exhaustion, both sides battled hand to hand—spear against bayonet. Dozens of bodies lay where they'd fallen, white beside black, with little crimson rivers running from each down onto the hard African soil.

Mastodon's steam whistle pierced the air, and Durnford's men gave us three hurrahs. The Zulus looked up at our approach, but none appeared frightened this time. They disengaged from their combat and ran to gather in some sort of formation up ahead of our elephant. Every now and then we heard the clang of a spear against Mastodon's iron hide. The noise of rhythmic chanting and shield-beating reached my ears.

Munro, Hood, and I aimed and fired our rifles through forward-facing slits in the drawing room. Lady Munro kept us supplied with fresh ammunition.

"By Jove, they're retreating! Got them on the run now," the Colonel said. "Onward, Mastodon! Let's have at them!"

Retreating? I wondered. Why would retreating warriors waste energy by chanting? Everything I'd seen of these Zulus pointed to purposeful action, determination, and discipline.

Our carriage lurched forward, then stopped.

Thrown to the floor by the sudden halt like the rest of us, Captain Hood scrambled to his feet first and peered out his slit. Above the noise of cheering Zulus, I heard a shrill whistling, increasing in pitch.

"What the devil?" Hood said, "Mastodon is—"

A tremendous explosion threw us to the floor again.

I had an impression of intense light blazing through the open slits, and then the room filled with dust and soot.

◉　◉　◉

As if in a daze, I rose and stumbled about. My head ached from an impact with something hard and my arms bled from a showering of glass fragments. As the dust cleared, I helped Lady Munro to her feet and made my way through debris to where Colonel Munro lay moaning.

"Sir, are you well?"

"Never better, Maucler. Thanks." But he winced as he stood up.

"My eyes!" Captain Hood sat rubbing his eyes and blinking. "I can't see a bloody thing." The heat and glare of the explosion had blinded the poor man. I knew then that our expedition's Orion, our Nimrod, might never hunt again.

With trepidation, I peered through a slit. The donga lay before me. Metallic wreckage lay all about its banks. Bodies of Zulus littered the scene.

A Zulu warrior's face appeared just before me, his necklace of bones jangling. He shouted and I recoiled.

"They're right outside! Shut the slits!" I hurried to close the openings on my side while the Colonel and his wife shut the others before anyone could cast a spear inside.

"We're trapped," I said.

"Then we fight to the last man," Colonel Munro reached for his pistol.

The forward door to the veranda, already bent from the explosion, burst open. Before the Colonel could get off a shot, several warriors rushed in, pushed each of us to the floor, and held spears to our necks. They took our weapons, motioned for us to stand, and prodded us out the door. Munro went with his wife, and I led the blind Captain Hood by the hand.

Devastation and carnage met my gaze. Not one of Durnford's troops remained alive. Zulu warriors busied themselves with stripping clothes from the dead and disemboweling the bodies, a gruesome practice I later learned was their custom. I saw smoke rising to the west, and feared the worse for Colonel Pulleine and the Isandlwana camp.

Our conquerors had captured the occupants of the second Steam House carriage as well, and they joined us on the ground beside the ruins of Mastodon. Goûmi and Sergeant McNeil both showed great relief at seeing the Colonel and Lady Munro alive. Fox, who'd suffered a shoulder wound, looked after Captain Hood. Our cook, Parazard, and our African guide, Tongané, appeared unharmed.

Of the three occupants of Mastodon, not much remained.

Warriors bound our wrists behind us and led us on foot toward the camp.

"What in bloody hell happened back there?" Munro demanded of nobody in particular.

No one else spoke for a time. "If I may, sir," I said, "I believe the Zulus lured us into the donga. Mastodon must have fallen partway into the ditch. Somehow his trunk may have become damaged, perhaps by striking the other side, pinching it closed. That left no way out for the expanding gases, and his boiler exploded."

He nodded and walked on in silence for a time. "Damn shame about Banks."

I shook my head. How could he forget about the brave stoker and engineman who'd accompanied us through both India and Africa? "Kâlouth and Storr were in there too."

"Yes, of course. Shame about them too."

At the camp beside Isandlwana Mountain, we beheld a horrible sight. Red-coated bodies lay strewn about while the Zulu victors performed their disgusting post-battle ritual on the dead and wounded. Wagons and tents stood ablaze, while some Zulus picked through British supply crates seeking valuables.

"My God," Sergeant McNeil said, "all of them, dead."

Spears poked at our backs and urged us to walk to the east. Surrounded by an escort of several dozen Zulus, we could talk among ourselves, but the chance of escape seemed remote.

Marching by foot over rocky terrain in the heat of an African summer proved much more trying than riding along in the Steam House had. Stripped of our technology, we found ourselves reduced to the level of the Zulus themselves. Worse, perhaps, since our captors—who surpassed us in overall physical fitness – seemed unfazed by the strenuous hike. The aged Colonel and the blind Captain fared the worst of us. Lady Munro got along well, and never strayed from her husband's side.

"Tongané," I asked our guide, "can you ask them where we're going?"

He spoke to the warriors in their language but I understood their one-word reply without translation: Ulundi, capital city of Zululand. What had Lord Chelmsford said, Ulundi lay some sixty five miles away?

"Please ask them why we were spared when so many others were killed."

After a brief exchange, Tongané said, "Orders of King Cetshwayo. Elephant Warriors to be brought to him unharmed."

So Mastodon had saved us, after a fashion. Now we marched toward a rendezvous with this nation's leader. A "corrupt Zulu warlord," Chelmsford had called him, a "belligerent, bloodthirsty bastard." What would this king do with us? I couldn't help but think that perhaps Banks, Kâlouth, and Storr had been the lucky ones.

◉　◉　◉

Three days later, I awoke to find a cockroach crawling on my nose. I swatted it away and propped myself on one elbow to look around. I lay on a woven grass mat, near where the eight other members of the Steam House party still slept. Together we filled most of the available space within a large, dome-shaped hut. Thatching, interlaced with a network of branches, formed the material for the hut, the whole thing supported by a central pole. Armies of cockroaches swarmed on the hut's walls, causing me to shiver with revulsion. Smoke lingered in the air, sole reminder of a fire that must have burned in the hut's crude hearth until dying during the night. A single door let some daylight in, an opening so low that we would have to scramble out on hands and knees.

Though every muscle screamed with soreness, I crawled in silence to the door. Through it I saw that many other similar huts surrounded a circular pen in the center, an enclosure for cattle bordered by low walls of grass and woven saplings. As soon as I started to exit, a pair of crossed spears barred my way, stabbed in the ground by Zulu guards just outside our hut. I decided instead to retreat back to my mat and wait for the others to awaken.

Somehow we'd all survived the forced march to Ulundi. Fox had gone delirious in the heat, Hood had sprained an ankle, and all of us suffered from fatigue and heat exhaustion. Colonel Munro had almost died. We'd taken turns supporting him while he passed in and out of consciousness.

Our captors had braved the journey with no apparent ill effects. Perhaps for them, a sixty-five mile trek through the African summer was something they could have done on the run, without even stopping. I marveled at the ease and lightness with which their army traveled. Compared with Lord Chelmsford's difficulties transporting men, horses, oxen, and wagons, the Zulus seemed much more agile and maneuverable. Little wonder that many thousands of warriors could appear as if from nowhere.

Two hours later the rest of our party awoke. A Zulu woman brought us water, berries, and cooked bushpig meat. While we breakfasted and regained some measure of strength, the conversation drifted from our pains and injuries, alit upon our imprisonment in a roach-infested hut, and finally stopped altogether.

"I just now remember reading," I said, "of a Frenchman named Lartet, I think, who discovered evidence of antediluvian man within some caves in southwestern France. There he found mastodon bones and stone spearheads."

"Is this how you make conversation, Maucler, or is there a point of interest in there somewhere?" Hood's jibe drew a few tired chuckles.

"Only this," I answered. "Somehow these primeval humans must have banded together to attack the mightiest beasts on Earth using only simple weapons. Similarly, our Zulu enemies faced a threat far beyond their understanding and found a way to defeat it. They lured us into that donga, probably hoping our elephant would at least become stuck or damage a leg."

"And they were lucky," Munro's voice sounded scratchy and weak. "I think you credit them with too much intelligence."

Nods from the other Europeans (except our French negro cook, Parazard) showed their agreement with this sentiment.

"I wouldn't dismiss them so readily, Colonel," I countered. "We've seen their zeal and discipline in battle. We've seen their hunting skill during the march here. Consider this. What would have happened if Africa and Europe had switched human populations a millennium ago? Both continents have natural resources, but Africa lacks navigable rivers and protected coastal seaport areas. These features foster trade, which develops civilizations. Without the benefits of trade, maybe primitive white Africans might now be facing a Mastodon invented and driven by European blacks."

"You're saying they'd be our equals, but for an accident of geography? Preposterous!" Munro's outburst brought on a fit of coughing.

"Perhaps," I said, "but I must point out that *we're* the ones in prison."

◎ ◎ ◎

I cannot say that the Zulu prison was comfortable, but neither can I state that our captors mistreated us. Every few hours, our guards allowed us out of the hut into the kraal. The guards seemed unconcerned about escape attempts, maybe because they could outrun us with ease. Women brought food– the 'monkey bread' fruit of the baobab tree, berries, nuts, and a variety of meats including hartebeest, blesbok, duiker, and reedbuck.

On our fourth day in prison, the guards brought us before the king, our hands bound behind our backs. I steeled myself for the encounter, determined to face death with bravery.

King Cetshwayo kaMpande sat on a fiber mat beneath one of the few trees in Ulundi. A large man with a round face and an intense gaze, he wore no emblems of royalty other than a dark, plaid sheet worn toga-fashion. Lines near his eyes hinted at a jovial spirit, while the lines across his forehead traced the worries of a nation's king.

He stared at each of us in turn, his mood indecipherable. At last he pointed at Colonel Munro and spoke.

"You are leader of iron elephant tribe," Tongané translated the King's words.

Munro nodded.

To my surprise, the King smiled and actually laughed. When he stopped, a conversation ensued with Tongané continuing to translate.

"It was a fine elephant. A great warrior beast."

The Colonel nodded without smiling.

"One day, maybe in the time of my son's sons, Zululand will have iron warrior elephants too."

I stood in awe of his audacity. From spears to steam traction engines in just two generations! Could it be possible?

Two of the men, perhaps McNeil and Fox, guffawed at the remark. In an instant, guards held spears to their necks.

With a single wave from the King's hand, the guards backed away. "You think me insane," Cetshwayo went on. "But I see a time when Zulu and English may be friends. We will trade. We give you things you want. You give us things we want, like iron elephant."

"Tongané, remind him that our countries are at war." The

Colonel wore a stern expression.

I did not think it wise to provoke the one who held our lives in his hands. I waited in trepidation for what might come next.

The King smiled. "Wars always end. After this war, I may travel to meet Great White Queen, and she will visit me as well."

I tried to imagine King Cetshwayo at Buckingham Palace with Queen Victoria, but could not.

He continued. "In time I will forget English invasion of Zulu-land, and we will live as friends."

Munro shut his eyes and clenched his teeth, perhaps fighting down some rash impulse. "I cannot deny that we invaded your land," he said, "but why did you ignore the ultimatum of the High Commissioner?"

The King frowned. "English paper say I must break up Zulu army. We are warrior people. It is our way. No army mean no Zulu. Did I send paper telling White Queen to break up *her* army? No! You English gave me choice—stop being Zulu, or fight. If you were King of Zululand, what would *you* do?"

◎　◎　◎

For over five months we remained in prison. Once we accepted the primitive nature of this life, we found it bearable, even comfortable, after a fashion. Our health improved, even that of Colonel Munro. He spent much time talking to King Cetshwayo, learning about the Zulu people and their army.

On July 4th, British forces, reinforced from England, overran and captured Ulundi, and freed us. The Anglo-Zulu War had ended. Yet, after having conquered Zululand, the British carved it up into thirteen separate kingdoms and withdrew. Commissioner Frere's policies in the region now discredited, the Empire abandoned the land it had won at such cost.

After being sent into exile, King Cetshwayo had no chance to realize his dream of owning an iron elephant. In my view, it is fortunate that the knowledge required to design and construct mechanized war vehicles like Mastodon died along with Banks. For the future, it seems, land warfare belongs to the horse-mounted cavalry and the foot soldier.

Some time after returning home, my friends invited me to London for a ceremony where we each received a Zulu War Campaign Medal. Though a posthumous award, Banks received the Victoria Cross. As we walked in silence along the river with the Colonel and Lady Munro back to their residence, he halted and turned to me. "I say, Maucler, you were right to question that bloody war. All those Zulus wanted was to be left alone, to live free and hunt in the wide-open spaces." He gestured in disgust at the carriages clogging the street, the belching smokestacks, and the crowds coming and going. "Confound it, I'm in a worse prison now that I've been rescued! And for our service in that fiasco, they gave us *these.*"

He removed his campaign medal from around his neck. The silver plated medallion depicted a crouching lion on one side and Queen Victoria on the other. Dangling it from its yellow and blue ribbon, Munro said, "All the medals in the Kingdom aren't worth the life of *one* of those brave chaps who died at Isandlwana. Kâlouth, Storr, and Banks, this is for you!" In one swift motion, surprising for an old man, he flung his medal far out into the Thames where it made a small splash, and disappeared.

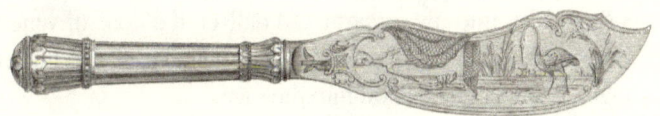

Doc Borden's Hard-Luck Hoss

Julie Frost

My horse squealed, reared, bucked, and pitched me headfirst into a giant yellow-flowered prickly-pear patch. I landed face-to-face with an enormous buzzing rattlesnake and understood why my usually-placid gelding had gone suddenly loco.

The rattler's head was bigger than my fist. Panic drenched my pores with sweat. I scrambled desperately to escape, but the rattler struck far more quickly than any human could dodge. Its fangs sank deep into my forearm and delivered a dose of venom that burned on contact. Tail still rattling, it pulled back and flicked its tongue before slithering off into the sage.

My horse, the traitor, stampeded away before I could catch him up.

I pulled the bandana from my neck with shaky fingers and used it to tourniquet my arm, a futile act of desperation. The nearest town lay days away on foot, too far to make before I succumbed to the poison in my blood. I had to try, though, didn't

I? I heaved myself upright and started that way, the hammer of the midday sun beating a relentless refrain on the anvil of my back.

In a short span of time, my arm swelled and turned black, the skin sloughing away to expose decaying muscle. Fiery pain radiated from the bite, racking my entire body with agony. Over the course of the day, and into the next, my walk slowed to a stumble, then a crawl. I faded in and out, my awareness settling into a concentrated pinpoint of *get to town.*

Delirious with fever, I finally collapsed in the dubious shade of a skeletonized cedar bush beside a greenish, poisoned water-hole. Scattered animal bones littered the vicinity—along with the freshly-expired body of my former mount, croaking vultures ripping at its swollen belly. I was incredibly thirsty, my canteen having run out after less than a day, but that water would kill me far faster than the snakebite. Part of me longed for a quick death, but the rotten-egg-and-tar stink was enough to keep me away.

The soft clop of walking hooves in dirt drew near. A shadow loomed over me. At first I thought a mustang had wandered by, but no wild bronc was this shining white, sporting a spiral horn in the middle of its forehead.

Clearly, I was hallucinating.

The beast blew through its lips, sniffing my face, chest, and arm, warm breath ghosting over me. It made a noise down in its throat—and touched the tip of the horn to the snakebite.

A pleasant tingle suffused my body, and I stared in fascination as the blackness across my skin retreated and the wound knit before my eyes, leaving smooth and unmarked flesh behind. I sat up and flexed my fingers, which moved freely for the first time since the bite. The critter tilted its head, regarding me from trusting brown eyes. And then it curled up beside me, laying its head in my lap with a contented sigh.

I reached out my hand, hesitating before straightening the forelock around that lethal-looking horn and touching the long face. If this was a hallucination, it was an awfully tactile one. The pain had disappeared like mist before a morning sun, and I wondered if I was dead. But neither singing angels nor horned demons arrived to escort me to the afterlife. I was alone with this remarkable, otherworldly creature lying peacefully at my side.

After a few moments, the other miseries of the situation impinged on my awareness. My mouth was dry and foul-tasting, with nothing to swallow down my equally dry throat. As if sensing my discomfort, the critter lifted its head and gracefully rose to its feet. It walked over to the waterhole and touched its horn to the surface, causing the murky water to shimmer from that point and then clear all the way to the bottom. The stink receded, replaced by the scent of a meadow after a rain.

I crept forward, salt and alkali crumbling beneath my knees, and lowered my face to drink. It was the coolest, sweetest water I'd ever tasted, and it restored me to full strength as I gulped my fill. After I sated my thirst, I was struck by a thought that froze me to the spot.

The horn *healed.*

If only I'd had it with me on the Civil War battlefields I'd left back east. My medical training hadn't done much good in the face of carnage like that. But with that horn, the possibilities were staggering. I turned them over in my head while I studied the creature more closely.

She was female, and I decided to call her 'Luna' because her soft radiance reminded me of the moon. She indicated no desire to take her leave, and even allowed me to examine her teeth and feet. Other than that extraordinary horn and the glow, she was a perfectly normal horse with hairy fetlocks and hooves that had never seen shoes.

The horn. I kept coming back to that. It had healed the snake-bite and turned a poisoned waterhole pure. I wondered if Luna would allow me to borrow her, in essence, to help my patients.

First, however, I had to get to town, which was still a couple of days away on foot. Would she let me ride her? After shooing the vultures away, I pulled the tack off my dead gelding and approached her with the saddle, talking in a soothing manner all the while. She waited placidly while I saddled her, like she'd been doing it all her life, but she didn't like the bit, so after some consideration I rigged the bridle as a hackamore instead. When I mounted up and clicked my tongue at her, she trotted obediently in the direction I steered.

I felt truly blessed. Things were looking up for the first time since I'd left Appomattox.

She took me to a decent-sized Colorado mining town without a noise of complaint or objection. The folks who lived there were only too happy to have a doctor move in, even if he was accompanied by a shiny horse with a horn in the middle of her forehead.

Luna was devoted to me, her affection more like that of a dog than a horse, and I returned it wholeheartedly. She'd saved my life, after all. I talked to her the same way I'd talk to a person, and there were times I swore she understood.

She allowed children to take shocking liberties with her. They played around her feet, pulled her tail, and rode her bareback with nary a care. But she received everyone else with the ferocity of a tiger, especially the saloon girls. She'd get a glint in her eye and bare her teeth, shaking her mane, if a woman approached too close for her liking. I didn't mind overmuch. One disastrous romance in my youth had spoiled me for female entanglements long ago, and the simple life of a bachelor suited me.

To my disappointment, her devotion to me and her hostility to others meant using the horn to help patients was a non-starter. She'd as soon stab them as look at them, as I discovered the first time I tried to coax her into touching her horn to a miner who came to me with a bad cough. I managed to stop her killing him, but only just. He scrambled inside and slammed the door shut behind him while I calmed Luna in front of my house.

Once I was sure she was all right, I went inside and gave the shaken miner my old standby cough remedy, which consisted of a mixture of molasses, honey, white wine vinegar, and laudanum. "Oh, Luna," I scolded her, exasperated, after he left. She bumped me with her nose and wuffled, while I eyed the horn and wondered idly what would happen if I took it from her.

That's all it was, at that point. Idle speculation.

I didn't have to wonder if the horn would heal anyone but me. The town children came down with the usual maladies and injuries, and she allowed me to bring them to her with no fuss. They walked away healed, even from such things as broken bones, or pox. It was nothing short of miraculous.

And we needed a miracle, I thought a few days later, staring grimly down at Karl Ryan, who ran the dry goods store. He'd been crossing the street when an out-of-control stagecoach careened around a corner and ran him over. One of his four young children came running for me, out of breath and sobbing. I mounted Luna bareback and raced to the scene of the accident.

Karl's wife was sickly; her last childbirth had nearly killed her and she'd never quite recovered. She couldn't run the store by herself if he died, nor could she take care of the kids alone. In desperation, I looked to Luna, but she shook her mane warningly at anyone who came too near her.

Karl was drowning in his own blood, right in front of me. I'd seen far too many injuries like this on the battlefield. Swallowing hard, I stood up and said, "I'll be right back. Don't follow me. Luna, come." Ignoring questions and carrying my medical bag, I took her into an alleyway between the dry goods store and the saloon.

I needed that horn.

I'd grown up on a ranch. De-horning cattle was a straight-forward operation, so I had no reason to think that de-horning Luna would harm her. I delved into my medical kit, which included a much-used-and-abused bone saw.

I settled into a cross-legged sit, remembering how Luna had rested her head in my lap the first time. She did it again, and I stroked her calmingly, running my fingers up and down that wondrous spike. "I'm sorry," I choked, grasping her horn firmly. I was *efficient* with the saw—three strokes and the horn was off.

Luna let out a pained cry, jerking away, her blood jetting out over my hands and shirt. "Easy, easy," I said, grabbing my kerchief and pressing it to the wound. Stupid, should have remembered it would do that. She laid her head back across my legs and wheezed. I caressed her neck and face, murmuring, keeping her calm, hoping she'd forgive me.

Her glow faded, slightly, but I didn't think anything of that. Not until later.

The bleeding soon stopped. I wished I had more time to comfort Luna, but Karl was dying—I might have already taken too long. Breathing a last apology to her, I raced back to my patient with the horn in my hand—

And touched the tip of it to his chest.

For a long moment, nothing happened, and I despaired, thinking I'd disfigured Luna for nothing. But then he inhaled, without that horrible death-rasp, his broken arms and legs flexing back to normal. It had worked.

"Doc, what'd you do?" one of the saloon girls asked, pointing at the horn. Luna chose that moment to shoulder her way through the crowd and bump my back with her nose. I looked up at her and noted with guilt the slight trickle of blood running down her forehead.

"What I had to," I answered. With leaden steps, I took her home.

She forgave me, though I didn't deserve it.

◎　◎　◎

At first, I used the horn for every illness they came to me with, but as time passed, I started noticing that it took longer to work the more I used it—and Luna was growing peaked and poorly, though her decline was gradual. I tried touching her with the horn, but it didn't perk her up even a tiny bit, which I thought was a shame, since it belonged to her in the first place. I stopped using it for anything but emergencies. Her ribs showed, and her coat dulled, until she resembled any other white horse you'd see in a livery stable. The farrier found nothing wrong other than a general failure to thrive.

The wound on her forehead never did heal.

We carried on normally for many years. The town boomed for awhile, then busted as the gold ran out. Then someone found a vein of silver, and the boom started again. As was usual in such-like circumstances, the boom brought unsavory elements in. The sheriff couldn't always corral them.

I was riding home one night after a late call out to a ranch, eyes tired and gritty, not paying as much attention as I ought. A man dressed in dark clothing, riding a black horse, came charging up the trail at me with such urgency that I figured he needed my help. I stopped Luna and hailed him.

Turned out he was nothing but a human rattlesnake. He pulled a six-shooter and aimed it square at my chest. "You're the doctor," he growled, "and I reckon you's a rich man. Hand over what money you got on you and tell me where you've stashed the rest, and you might live."

I got indignant, which probably wasn't the best course of action. He barely let me get a sentence out before his gun roared and something punched me in the chest, sending me tumbling off Luna's back to land in the dust, blood bubbling up my throat.

Luna let out an enraged roar, a sound I'd never heard a horse make in my life, and charged the bandit. His mount turned to flee of its own accord, but she was on them before it got more than a couple of steps. She leaped high and landed in the middle of its back. It collapsed under her weight with a spine-cracked grunt and didn't move again.

Luna scrambled to her feet, ears flat against her head, teeth bared, intent on finishing the bandit. She snaked her head forward to take a hunk out of him while he attempted to crawl away. He wasn't moving too well, and I automatically cataloged his injuries—broken leg and ribs, at the least. Her jaws snapped again and again, front and rear feet lashing at him too, and he let out ungodly screeches as she tore him up.

But I had more urgent concerns, such as the bullet that had blown through my lung and out my back. My vision dimmed. I couldn't breathe. "Lu...Luna," I managed.

Her head whipped around, and she galloped over to me, lowering her head to snuffle at my profusely-bleeding chest. I raised my hand and stroked her nose, once. "I'm sorry," I said.

"I'm sorry...I hurt you."

She snorted and dropped to her knees, pressing her scabbed forehead, where the horn had been, to my wound. "Luna, no–" I started. Too late.

She'd healed me again. And then that faithful animal, whom I'd wronged so horribly all those years ago, crumpled the rest of the way to the ground and breathed her last.

When the townsfolk followed the bandit's trail back to us, they found me sitting with Luna's head cradled in my lap, bawling like a baby.

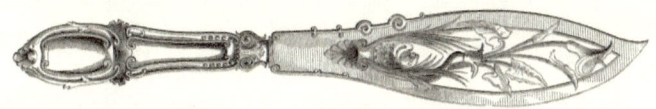

GENTLEMANLY HORRORS OF MINE ALONE

DONALD J. BINGLE

"Well played," muttered Rogers, the majordomo of the Wanderers' Club, amidst the gentlemanly utterances of "Good show," "Here, here," and even "Huzzah" as Sir Algernon Hogshead finished his tale with a dramatic flourish.

Though not so socially gregarious as to partake in the verbal bonhomie, I thumped my ivory serpent's-head cane a few times, myself, in collegial support of my frenetic friend as his bizarre, but well-told, tale had come to its breathtaking and remarkable conclusion. Truth told, the hubbub of excited utterances and exclamations regarding Sir Hogshead's fanciful quest were well-said, but, greater truth yet, I had become more and more pensive and apprehensive as the tale progressed.

I knew what was coming next. Not within the story, but after.

The roiling cloud of despair and embarrassment to come darkened my already disquieted disposition.

I looked down at the ancient Oriental carpet beneath my

wing-backed leather chair in an attempt to distract myself from the obligation soon to come to me, focusing on the rug's pattern to find the intentional flaw that would identify the village which had woven it. Finding flaws aplenty in myself, but none discernible in the carpet, I abandoned the trivial quest and gave the brandy in my heavy crystal snifter a languid swirl to release more of its richly intoxicating scent. As an expectant silence seeped in to replace the boisterous utterances of only a few moments before, I looked up to meet the gazes of my fellow club-members as they turned toward me.

Though my chair was the closest of any to the fireplace and its rolling waves of rough, dry heat, I suppressed a shudder. Someone near the snooker table cleared his throat with a rumbling cough and Throckmorton, to my right, tapped his pipe sharply to clean out the ashes before refilling.

I screwed up my courage to at least speak—that I had barely enough courage to do so was part of my despair and my shame.

"Gentlemen," I said, holding my voice steady and doing my best to hold my drink steadier yet, so as to not betray my trepidation. "Though not of the experienced years of some of you, and only recently returned from my sojourn abroad in the Americas, I know the traditions of the Wanderers' Club, as did my father and his father before me. Wherever gentlemen gather to smoke and relax and drink and socialize, whether in a men's society or an adventurer's guild or the parlor of the main keep of a country castle after a hearty meal of fresh-killed venison, the routine is familiar. Tales are told, one by one, to the gathered collegium: tales of exploration and derring-do; tales of adventure and heroic quest; tales of far-off places and strange...sometimes very strange...ways."

I held the snifter to my nose, breathing in the pungent aroma to steel my nerves. "The tales are told to amaze and delight, to educate and inspire, to boast of prowess in the understated way a man may do among his fellows without shame, and to establish one's place of belonging, even of honor, within the confines of gentlemanly society."

I felt the snifter begin to quiver and set it down upon the adjoining table, as quickly as I believed would look natural. "My turn has come and I have no excuse for not telling you my tale. Having recently returned from extensive travels in that wild continent across the Great Atlantic, I cannot say with veracity that I have no new adventure to impart. And though there are in clubs such as ours, occasional whispers of exaggeration and embellishment by those whose natural skills of oratorical flourish have been augmented and encouraged by the strong spirits conjured by master craftsmen of distilled liquors, I cannot in honor tell you, my brethren, an untruth."

I rubbed my hand across the faint stubble of my chin, releasing by such touch a waft of the sweet, musky scent of my men's cologne. I fixed my hand to my chin a moment to steady my hand's growing shake, before lowering it to my side, shifting my jacket out of the way, and hitching my thumb into the watch pocket of my vest—as they are prone to do in the western regions of America, where vests are often worn without a proper jacket.

"I am shamed to admit that mine is not a tale of derring-do and wondrous things, but sadly a tale, as it were, of derring-don't and unspeakable things. But it is my tale and my shame—mine alone—and I hope that you will take what caution you can from it."

I took a deep breath and began in earnest, my nerves steadying as the words poured forth and memories too long held in were set free.

"Like all great tales, mine involves a woman, a treasure, and great danger. As you know, my family's fortune is built upon railroading and even a man of wealth and leisure must occasionally tend to matters mercantile. That my inspection of the factories and foundries of our Americas division should neces-sitate travel to that rugged and bounteous land to see its great expanses and wondrous, unspoilt vistas was, to me, a fortuitous benefit of great interest. And so, I took the train to Southampton and shipped out in as much luxury as ocean-travel permits to sail to the Americas.

"I landed in New York and took care of needful business both there and in the rail capitals of the eastern seaboard generally, before making way west to Chicago and on to St. Louis, Topeka, and out Denver way. At each stop, I tended to business matters and introduced myself into the local social scene, as much as such rustic lands allow, enjoying the fine, warm days of summer after my cold spring voyage across the North Atlantic. It was autumn by the time I arrived in Denver and though the high plains were windy and chill, there was no snow yet to damp the festivity of that mile-high city, though a heavy, white blanket lay over the mountains looming to the west and southwest."

I leaned forward in the wing-backed chair to allow the radiant heat of the fire's glow to warm my sallow cheeks, which cooled with the memories of my visit to Denver and points west. "Feckless and consumed by my own frivolous pursuits in the city, I delayed my needful visit to the foothills of the great Rocky Mountains where I was tasked to assist with the engineering of a narrow gauge line to service the silver and gold mines that dot the hills of the region—mines so numerous the trees of the heavily forested hillsides have all been stripped bare to provide firewood, as well as timber supports for the working shafts and the mine trains servicing the gaping maws in the earth.

"I should not have delayed my journey. There was no reason to do so. For once I headed into the mountains, I discovered that the mine town in which I had my engineering task was sur- prisingly large and well-appointed, though a bit rugged and brash —as were its denizens. The engineering work itself was most interesting, occasioning a trestled loop of tracks winding about the outskirts of the mountain town so as to gain height within a confined area at an acceptable grade in order to make way farther west into the hills to the most active and profitable mine workings. The scenery, despite the devastation of the vegetation for as far as the eye could see, was still breathtaking—stark and white, the air a striking blue cut by vivid grey and white peaks, with puffs of white where the fiercely cold wind swept up powdery snow crystals to form graceful drifts in the swales below."

I closed my eyes and saw the scene in my mind's eye and then my memory shifted to an even more beauteous view, my beloved

Vivian. My eyes misted and I paused as I fought to maintain control. Finally succeeding, I waved my free hand indifferently in front of my face, as if clearing a waft of errant smoke from the still roaring fire to my right.

"But enough travelogue. All was well as winter came strong and fast to our fine city. But all was better still, when I first met ...my lady friend. Gay, witty, and a sparkling conversationalist, my business had some undertakings with her husband's mining interests to the west. She so lit the room with her smile that kerosene lamps were scarce needed. She so entranced all about that conversation stopped and it was as if the pianist in the corner played only for your own pleasure. She so delighted all that I never heard an unkind word about her, not from servants or rivals or clucking wives or even coarse men from the mines.

"Alas, she was married, else a thousand swains wooing would lie at her feet. I, of course, treated her with honor and respect, despite the desires of my heart. But still, we became friends and as the winter deepened into frigid isolation I gave thanks to the heavens that I could enjoy her company for a few hours almost every day—as her husband remained at the western mines almost a day's ride away and she grew melancholy alone in her grand house all day."

I paused, lost in a reverie of her look, her voice, and her laughter as we told tales of our journeys and our lives, until a voice from across the room broke my trance of misgiving: "The treasure, man. You said there was treasure." "Yes," came another voice, this one close and gruffer. "And danger, too."

I smiled as the impatience and priorities of my colleagues showed themselves. "Ah, yes," I replied. "I did promise both and, as is usually the case, they arrived together nigh unto dawn one February morn. One of my...friend's...manservants rousted me from my slumbers by loudly pounding on the door to my quarters in a fine hostelry. He held out a note on folded lavender stationary that smelled of gardenias in the spring. *Please come quickly with my servant. I am in need of your assistance.* The note was unsigned, no doubt to maintain propriety if it were to fall into unintended hands, but I was of no uncertainty whatsoever as to who sent it and what I must do. I dressed straight-away and bundled up for a journey in the cold, bringing along a pack of supplies and my never-fired Colt Peacemaker revolver, which I had acquired in Topeka during a boring stopover in my earlier travels. So provisioned, I rushed as quickly as possible to offer whatever needful assistance I could to my dear friend."

Another shiver came upon me, and I took a quick swallow of my brandy, more for warmth than taste, before continuing my tale.

"Every window of the grand home blazed with light as we approached, the manservant throwing open the door without knocking. As we entered the foyer, I heard a wail and a thump, and before I could scarce react, much less remove my bulky outer garment, my friend flew into my arms, burying her head in my shoulder, distraught beyond measure. Several pieces of paper were clutched in her hand, crumpled by her rigid grip.

"The manservant excused himself and somehow we made it into the parlor, where a fire built so high as to threaten to soften the andirons blazed brightly It took several minutes, but finally her sobbing spasms lessened sufficiently she could speak.

"'Please, my lady,' I said. 'Tell me what malady has befallen you and I will do whatever may be required to allay your distress.' Her gaze darted up toward mine own, then flitted to the pages she held, then to the windows, where the heat of the fireplace was doing battle with the frost caused by the frigid conditions a mere pane away. 'What dire communication have you received that frights you so?'

"Her red-rimmed eyes filled with tears anew and the hand holding the crumpled pages began to quiver without control. 'From whence comes this missive?' I asked.

"'From the west, from the mines...' she whispered in reply.

"'From your husband?'

"She shook her head 'no' and once again gazed toward the frost attempting to re-assert itself upon the blackness of the window pane. As if in response, the glass rattled as a blast of cold assaulted it. She looked down toward the floor, as if ashamed by her next words: 'From the mine foreman. It appears my husband is lost.' Why such words should embarrass her, I could not say. Rather than reply, I reached out and took the pages from her trembling grip. When she made no protest, I intruded upon her personal correspondence without apology and read the communication itself.

"I am stricken with grief to write with such dreadful tidings, my lady, but I know not what else to do. All is not well at the mine. Winter has set in with a fearful vengeance here at these higher altitudes. Snow after snow after snow has visited the camp, piling high above the rooftop of even the mill and forestalling work of any kind above the ground. Many of the workers abandoned the camp as the weather worsened, until there were too few of us left to efficiently work the mines, even if the last large group to depart had not broken into the storeroom and taken most of the remaining food supplies to provision their flight from this place. Perhaps they were the wise ones to leave when they did, but we all curse them for leaving little behind. We cannot hunt. Each new snow is greater than the one before and is broken only by bouts of the fiercest cold I have ever known. Finally, those of us left, your husband included, retreated into the mine for shelter and relative warmth, carrying what meager provisions remained. That was a week ago. As the cold increased, we went further and further into the mine, but with poor ventilation and nothing to burn but the shoring timbers and rail planks, our lot was dark and miserable and we grew desperate and hungry.

"Your husband did his best to provide for both our physical well-being and our morale, taking the smallest portions of our meager fare, venturing into the lower levels with canteens to fetch clear, clean water, and telling us tales of his sundry exploits as a miner and a businessman. Though his offerings provided little in the way of real sustenance, we were thankful for his efforts until three days ago.

"He returned from his daily trek for water much later than usual, the stub of his torch barely flickering to light his way and the canteens empty of liquid. He arrived with great excitement,

raving about how, as he had approached the area where he regularly retrieved water, he had come upon the tracks of a great beast. In hopes of locating a bear which had ventured for a refreshing drink just before entering into its hibernating slumber, he had tracked the creature. The lengthy trail led out of the mine workings into natural tunnels beneath the earth, until it opened up into a large cavern.

"His story was strange. Surely there are bears in these mountains and they do, no doubt, hibernate to escape the frigid winter, but to find one so far and so deep from ground level was perplexing, yet he asserted it with great fervor. When, however, he began to describe the creature's lair as filled with gold, coins littered upon the floor, necklaces and gems scattered about, and the like, we realized he had gone quite mad from the privations and cold he had endured. His words were fevered and, we discovered, so was his brow.

"Doing our utmost to tamp down our incredulity, we attempted to humor him, to mollify him concerning his ravings over the treasure and the mythical beast which must have gathered it, but the effort was most difficult. After all, bears are not magpies; they do not collect shiny objects. Hoards are the province of dragons, which are merely imaginary constructs found in children's tales. Despite doing our best to keep our doubts and concerns to ourselves, he must have sensed our disbelief, for while we later slept, he crept out of our makeshift camp with the last of our torches. When we discovered he was gone, we called out to him, but heard no response except our own echoes. We dared not follow without adequate light and so we sat and waited, straining for any sight or sound of his return.

"A day later we heard a distant scream of terror, which was cut off abruptly, yet echoed on in the mine shafts and in our minds. After another day's wait, we began to make our way back to the surface in the dark, the men feeling it better to take our chances in the snow and cold, than wait for death below the surface of God's earth. The way was slow and dark, but the main passage wide and straight. Eventually, we saw the light *glimmering through the cracks of the mine door. Once back at camp, we attempted to gather such supplies as remained by cutting through the roof to break into the mine office. Most of us are headed west, downslope a half-day to a competitor's mine camp, in the hope of food and salvation.*

"Jake, the bearer of this letter, has determined to take the longer trek east, as he is betrothed to the daughter of the local stableman and insists upon returning to her. He has agreed to bring this letter to you. Despite its tidings, I beg you show him the same nurture your husband attempted to his last to provide to all of us.

"My lady had composed herself during my reading of the crumpled pages, but as my eyes flicked back up to her at the finish, she looked upon me with a gaze of desperation. 'I beg of you,' she pleaded. 'You must find my husband. You must bring him back to me.'

"'Of course,' I replied without hesitation or, frankly, any coherent thought whatsoever. Some wags might say that I was reacting to her obvious distress, or that I sought the unbelievable treasure for myself, or that, lovesick as I have admitted myself to this assemblage to be for her, I knew that I could never have her love if I did not attempt to perform this quest, or, more calculating still, that I knew failure to find evidence of her husband's death would delay both my wooing of the fair lady and her receipt of her inheritance. But as members of the Wanderers' Club, I do not doubt you know the truth of what I am about to say: no man can deny such a request, despite the risks or rationality involved, and yet continue to call himself a man.

"My mind engaged itself upon the task at hand and began to formulate plans. 'I will need provisions ...'

"She interrupted: 'My servants have been preparing in greatest haste since the letter first arrived.'

"'...and I shall need to speak with Jake to find out more detail and, one prays, to convince him to accompany me to the mine and guide my endeavor.' I consulted my old pocket watch. 'I assume he has eaten. Has he rested also?'

"Her eyes fled back to the floor. She spoke in a whisper. 'He has not eaten. He is at rest, but not rested.'

"I furrowed my brow in confusion for but a moment before her next words raced my logic to a sad conclusion.

"'Jake was found by a trapper near the creek west of town, frozen to death. The undertaker found the letter in his clothing. No one's sure how long he's been dead or how long it took to get from the mine to the creek. This letter could be almost a fortnight old.'

"The direness of the situation pressed upon my mind—not just the risks of getting to the snowbound mining camp or the dangers of a dark, lonely trek through a massive labyrinth of adits and shafts, but the remoteness of any discernible outcome at all, much less a favorable one. Most likely, I would risk greatly and expend much effort to find nothing. Nevertheless, I expressed my condolences for forwarding to Jake's betrothed and set fast upon my preparations.

"Others at the Wanderers' Club have in their time told great tales of their journeys through the cold and ice and the dreary numbness of mind and body that comes from such travels. I shall not in any manner gainsay or belittle their achievements by dwelling on my own winter trek, except to say that I am not them. I had not their skill, nor their preparations, nor their physical and mental conditioning, nor their driving determination, and, so, my three-day journey was for me a bitter torture filled with icy stabs of pain, tempered by even more ominous creeping numbness.

"Upon arrival at the camp, I took shelter in the mine office, entering through the holed roof. I first located a map of the mine, then made a fire of things less useful. I slept until I woke naturally from the cold invading as the fire dimmed. It mattered not whether I would begin my quest underground during night or day—all within would be black within five minutes of entering the mine.

"The central adit—though some may refer to mines as tunnels, they are technically adits, as a tunnel is open on both ends and an adit open on merely one—was broad and well-constructed. So at first I proceeded with good speed, no longer encumbered by heavy drifts and howling winds. My provisions were calculated for my task. Of course, I carried food and water, but neither in overabundance. Water I knew I could find in the mine. Food was essential to maintain energy and body heat, but since I had no long-term concern for proper nutrition, adequate protein, or taste satisfaction, I carried primarily fats and sweets—fats for satiety and sugars for energy—most especially a large pot of sugar mixed with butter and ground coffee, along with hard candies to suck on while I moved.

"Light was my most important supply. I carried both oil lanterns (I could burn the sugared butter in a pinch) and tar-soaked torches, in as much quantity as I dared carry. In addition to providing heat, useful but not nearly as essential in the mine as it would be in the bitter cold of the high mountains in full winter, the light would allow me to track my progress via the mine map I carried and to search for tracks or other signs of passage that could lead me to the fictional lair accessed by way of the water source in the deep levels of the mine.

"It took less than a full day by my measure to find the 'camp' where the miners had taken refuge from the frigid cold outside. I rested there, eating and consulting my map and the tracks leading away, deeper into the mine. Part of me hoped that my lady's husband would come strolling up, filled canteens in hand, to greet me. Alas, such a fortunate and happy occurrence was not to be.

"I pressed on, slower now as I checked for tracks and consulted and amended the mine map as I progressed. I took every opportunity to go lower in the mine, my logic being that the water source was at a lower level and the shortest route to such water would have been the one chosen to replenish supplies. My methodical approach and a few inevitable blind alleys conspired to lead me to take almost ten hours to find the underground lake in a flooded section of the mine. Again I rested without slumbering, replenished my own water, forced enough gag-inducing buttered sugar and caffeine down my gullet to energize myself, and studied the many tracks near the edge of the water and the approaches to it.

"Along with the tracks of many booted feet, including my own, there were some bare tracks—as in unshod feet, not the creature. Though clawed, the tracks lacked the rounded pads associated with bears and other furred animals, and were clearly too large to be any other form of animal known to habitat mines, though I confess to being no expert on badgers and wolverines and other creatures of the Americas.

"My progress slowed even more as I tracked the strange trail, especially once I was far from the water and the ground was more firm and any residual mud on the footprints I was following well worn off. My only advantage in my tracking effort was that many passageways went for significant distance without intersecting with other passageways. With no opportunity for detours or changes in direction, I had only to analyze with vigor any junction area and, once I discerned the path—right, left, or forward—I could move again with speed for a little while.

"Despite the incredulity of the letter's tale of the pathway to the dragon's hoard, I took it as a good sign when the worked passage I was following gave way to a natural seam in the rocks. After a few hours of uneven, rock-strewn meandering, and in-creasingly confining and jagged walls twisting and turning about until I lost all sense of direction, I cursed nature and her ways. Instead, I prayed for any respite from the confusing array of incipient cave-in materials, whether a wide spot in which to stretch out a moment or a flat rock or space on which to sit.

"Finally, I found it: a flat ledge a bit less than a meter wide and almost two-meters long, waist-high along the right wall. I was tired beyond belief. I brushed off what little rocky debris littered the ledge and lay down upon it, curving my body to match the contours of the ledge. I took out my foodstuffs to rejuvenate myself before I rested, but was apparently too tired to eat. In retrospect, falling into a catatonic slumber, both arms hugging a pot of buttered sugar and coffee, was not my finest moment.

"The next moment I remember was even worse.

"I woke with a throbbing headache which was magnified by

the ear-splitting bellow of a huge, hideous beast. No doubt the headache was also accentuated by the fact that I was upside down, being carried in a swinging, haphazard way over the shoulder of such hideous beast, with my face bouncing along the hairy, fetid flesh of its naked buttocks. I dare say I would have screamed like a little Mary, joining in the cacophony of its own bestial yells, had it not been that even in my addled state I instinctively realized that nothing good was going to come of opening my mouth, or inhaling heartily so as to yell, in this unhappy position.

"Neither my condition nor my perspective provided a good vantage for a full description of the beast—all I could see through my slitted eyelids as I swung haphazardly to and fro was pale, scabby, flea-ridden, hairy skin and dried excrement. But from further examination during my confines in that dim-lit lair of despair, I can report to you assembled gentlemen that the creature was humanoid, almost three meters high, with pale, blotchy skin, long arms, long legs, and white and gray matted hair. The eyes were heavily recessed, small and black, the ears overly long and sharp-pointed like a canine's, but the nose flat and squat and snot-encrusted. The claws were more like long, sharpened nails—neither curved, nor apparently retractable. They were gray-black in color and broken and jagged. The stench of the creature was foul and most overpowering—I dare say I maintained consciousness partly because of its pungent irritation. The cavern itself stank of mildew. A small, yellow fire at the far end of the immense cavern threw off black, sooty smoke.

"I believe such is an adequate description of my environs, except for three things. First, and least, was the immense hoard of treasure."

I stopped my tale for a solid measure and looked about at the enthralled gaggle of club members. The single word "treasure" had immediately stilled and intensified the level of interest of the entire crowd—there was not a single incident of throat-clearing or shifting about or sipping or even swirling a drink until after I spoke again.

"The rough cavern walls were, themselves, streaked with

DONALD J. BINGLE 63

veins of gold, at least in the lower reaches where the soot of the constant fire had not blackened any variation away. The uneven floor was strewn with coinage, principally golden. Silver teapots, broken china, jumbled flatware, fancy candelabra, ornate mirrors, and flashy jewelry of all sorts and fashions were lying about in disorganized profusion. Given the remoteness of the location, I could only presume that this represented untold years' worth of booty from capturing and looting passing settlers, miners, trappers, traders, and supply convoys traveling over the nearby mountain passes. I even saw a few swords and pieces of military wear which appeared to be quite old."

Again, I looked at the assemblage, many now visibly leaning forward in their wanton greed to catch every syllable. One of the younger, more aggressive adventurers opened his mouth as if to speak, but I waved him off. "No, I won't tell you where the treasure hoard is located. You may have made note that I have avoided names of persons or places (other than those of great cities and first names most mundane) altogether. Though at times awkward to the telling of my tale, I wish to divulge nothing of substance. I shall give you no hint of the treasure's location, not even under the considerable pressure of my peers and the etiquette of our honored traditions. And, no, it is not because I covet the treasure for myself. First of all, you would not believe the location if I told you—that a treasure so large and old could be so close and so accessible to traveled ways. Second, in the event you did believe me, I will not tell you because such telling might impact on my beloved...lady friend...and I will not distress her any more than I already have. But third, and most important of all, I will not because if I do so, you will go there and see horrors unimaginable. Worse yet, you will go there and wish you had died. I cannot, in good conscience, do that to a fellow human being, much less a gentleman."

Whether to cover his gaffe or his greed, the middle-aged whippersnapper that had opened his mouth before my cautionary tirade, spoke up. "You said beyond the first there were two more features of the cavern you have not yet described." His prompt irked me, both in form and in substance. This was the hardest part of the tale to tell and although I had promised the group my confession, as it were, I realized I was stalling somewhat in getting to it. However, there is no time like the present, especially when you are ashamed of your past and have no future to look forward to.

"The second feature to which I referred was a deep pit, more than five meters from top to bottom, in which I was soon to become imprisoned. More of that anon. But the third feature was a more gruesome aspect of the cavern and the hoard. Along with the veins of gold and sooty residue, amidst the shiny trinkets and valuable artifacts from times gone by, there were bones and blood and rotting remains of meat and organs and skin. The whole room reeked of rancid death and maggot-ridden meat. Blood splatter stained the shiny surfaces of the scattered treasure, dark and dry. Mounds of hair and skin lay heaped wherever I turned my eyes in fear and despair. Cracked bones, the marrow sucked from the middle, lay discarded in piles of garish white. The beast not only robbed his victims of their shiny objects, he captured and slaughtered them and ate them raw.

"This club is a place of taste and refinement, so I shall not say more of that abattoir of evil, except to say that it made me more afraid than I have ever been or ever wish to be. Not for my life—for I knew in a single glance that I was likely doomed to be dinner, breakfast, lunch, and tea-time snack—but for my soul. For, you see, suicide is a mortal sin, but there was no way I was going to allow that...creature...to gnaw on me alive.

"Yet here I sit, in civilized company, a fine drink in my hand and a comfy chair at my backside, to tell the tale. This is the part where pluck and luck and physical skill and gallant bravery usually combine to save the day. I can only wish it were so.

"Instead, let me return to the pit, where I was soon to be held. It was a foul place, too, as you would imagine. Crusted with blood, with a floor of fine crushed bones and teeth, with walls too steep to climb. The thing is, it was not empty.

"At the bottom lay my lady's husband. Emaciated and scarcely breathing, I was amazed to find him still alive. More amazed still, when I approached him and discovered one of his arms had been torn or, worse yet, chewed off. His toes were also gone, and large chunks of meat had been ripped from his thighs and buttocks. I would have scarce recognized him from my lady's description—in such a state he was—but the logic of who he must be was undeniable. My conclusion was confirmed by the picture on the inside of his open pocket-watch of the gaily smiling visage of my dear, sweet friend. He had set the opened watch before his face before he lost consciousness, no doubt so as to have a last look at her before the end.

"When I saw that, I cried out. Not from the horror of that dreadful place, or the fear of what was to become of me, or even the tragedy of what had befallen my dying companion, but from shame—shame that I had flirted with my lady friend in her husband's absence, shame that I had lusted after her, shame that I had engaged in witty banter for my own amusement and appetites while her husband, albeit unbeknownst to us at the time, was being eaten alive by a beast beyond understanding.

"My lady's husband died about three days later, without ever regaining consciousness. It seemed like an eternity, but I measured the time in the dim, shadowed light by his watch, never moving it from his hand until he had passed, lest he wake and not find his beloved wife's visage there. The light dimmed further as time progressed and the fire in the cavern above waned—whether because the monster slept or had gone hunting, I did not know. But by the fourth day, I realized that I had heard nothing, but there was yet some light despite the fact the fire must no longer be burning. And that is when I realized there must be access to the outside near, and, accordingly, there was a glimmer of hope as well as of light.

"I seized upon that hope with all my being, feverishly making wild, crazed plans for how I would battle off the beast when it returned for me (for there was no way to climb the walls that held me in the pit), but as time passed and passed yet again, I came to a realization—that the monster had fed well and like many creatures of the wilds did not need to feed often. I had no food or water—the beast had taken my sugared butter. No doubt the smell of my provisions had led him to me. My hard candy was in my pack somewhere unknown, as was my virgin Colt. My strength was dwindling. By the time the creature came back, I would be too weak to fight.

"I could not let that happen.

"It would be easy to say I was delirious, mad with hunger and despair, but that would be a lie. Gentlemen, though they may do many things, do not lie to one another. And so I tell you true, I ate the only thing I had available to eat. I ate the object of my quest: my fair lady's husband. Not tentatively, mind you, not in little bits to maintain mere life. I ate all I could and waited a bit and then ate some more. I ate while the meat was still good. I ate while there was still hope to gain strength and battle the beast. I did what I believed must be done.

"And when the monster came to me, I feigned death. I lay limp until he hooked a rope around my ankle and pulled me up. Then, when he held me high, dangling me before his hideous face to savor his coming meal, I pulled out the two forearm bones that I had gnawed from my companion's body and sharpened by rubbing them against the smooth rock walls of the pit, and I plunged them into his black eyes and up into his brain.

"He fell.

"I lived.

"That is my tale."

To my right, Throckmorton sputtered as he half-rose from his chair. "But what of your lady, man? What did you tell her? How did she react?"

I stared at the old adventurer. Did he not understand anything at all about love?

"I told her nothing. I headed west. I never saw or communicated with her again."

The whippersnapper spoke up. "But why? You accomplished her quest. You found out what happened to her husband. Wouldn't she want to know?"

"Know what? That her husband died a gruesome, pain-wracked death for naught? That her would-be lover ate her husband's flesh with vigor to save his own miserable life? That I crave her in ways she can never know or understand? The shame is on me. I wish her no further harm. She is better off thinking us both dead. I would be better off if her belief was true."

I looked into my snifter, then downed the rest of the drink without pleasure. The crowd began to break up into smaller groups to discuss other, happier, adventures. I excused myself and made my way over to the bar, where Rogers tended things patiently.

He handed me two-fingers of single-malt in a heavy crystal tumbler without waiting to see what I ordered.

"Pardon my saying, Sir Ashton-Moore, but you left something out."

I gave him a hard look. "I did?"

"The beast," intoned the majordomo. "What was the beast?"

"The beast is dead. It is of no further consequence."

"I listen to a great many stories, m'lord. I have heard tales —sometimes, of course, second and third-hand—about creatures which revel in greed and seek out human flesh to eat. The native tribes in the Americas have several similar names for such creatures: Weendigo, Windiga, and Whitikow, among them."

I shrugged my shoulders. "The name is of no concern. The creature is dead."

Rogers' nose twitched. "It's just that I noticed you didn't have dinner tonight, like most of the gents. Drinks, yes, but nothing to eat."

I laughed aloud. "Rogers! A lot of gentlemen here drink with prodigious enthusiasm. It is hardly your place to warn me off, especially after you served me a drink moments ago without me even asking for one."

Rogers looked at me without smiling. "It's not the drinking, sir, that bothers me. It's the not eating in polite company."

I knew where he was going, but I had to keep up the pretense. "Whatever do you mean?"

"See, sir, the Weendigo, they do what they do because they're cursed by their past. They used to be human, but they're doomed to such fate by having succumbed to cannibalism in desperate times. The guilt, deserved or not, it causes them to change, to crave even more flesh, even more of what they can never have. And, should they succumb to these powerful urges, the human meat consumed infects them, causing them to change physically, even to putrefy alive. Most often the doomed souls are caught because they live hidden near a small population and are unable or unwilling to control their appetite. They just can't help themselves and take and take until they get noticed." Rogers picked up a clean glass and poured himself two fingers of the same single malt. "Your creature, he preyed on travelers—so he was around for a considerable time."

"Perhaps," I replied. "Most days I am too melancholy to think on it. And most evenings I am too ashamed to be in polite company."

"It's a sad tale, sir. That's the truth." He downed his drink in a quick pull. "Can I assume then, sir, that you'll be eating else-where tomorrow also?"

"Tomorrow night and every night I'm in town, I'm afraid, Rogers."

The majordomo wrinkled his nose as if catching a whiff of something unpleasant. "I'm not so sure, sir, you're the one who should be afraid."

Having accomplished what I came to do for the evening, I tipped Rogers generously and walked away toward the door of the Wanderers' Club, motioning to the doorman to hail a transom cab. As I waited, I pulled my pocket watch out, flipping it open to check the time. Vivian's face gazed up at me, beautiful and serene as always.

God, how I crave that woman. It's a good thing there is half a continent and an ocean between us.

Rogers was a good man. He would talk to the right club members discreetly and arrange for what must be done.

After all, suicide is still a mortal sin.

KUTSENKO'S CAGE
WILLIAM BURTON McCORMICK

1905, ODESSA

There were two remarkable things about Doctor Kutsenko:

He was the most handsome man Tasia ever knew.

And he owned a cage.

He and *it* arrived one sunny spring morning while Tasia was down at the market shopping, her usual habit as Mother was away working in Yalta. When Tasia returned to their family's lodging house past noon, she found her sister in a grand mood.

"We've a lodger," said Eleni before Tasia stepped two feet into the house. "Arrived an hour after you left."

"A lodger?" asked Tasia as she set her basket on the parlor table. "No more lodgers while Mother's away. Remember what happened with the last one?"

"He's a doctor. And very charming. I've given him the second-floor room."

"Eleni, we can't live unchaperoned with a man. The neighbors will think us a bordello."

"The neighbors *are* a bordello, Tasia."

"Yes, but..."

"And I'll wager even they don't pay four rubles a week."

"Four rubles a week?"

"In advance." Eleni withdrew the coins from her skirt pocket and presented them to Tasia.

"Four a week, my word..."

"Let me introduce you." Eleni gripped Tasia's hand and pulled her up the narrow stairwell to the second floor landing. There the door to the spare room stood open. Inside was a man of no more than thirty-five, well-dressed in a felt suit and sparkling black shoes. He stood at the bedroom dresser, atop of which he had laid the tools of a doctor's trade on handkerchiefs. His head bent down as he organized the instruments, Tasia could see a sun-bronzed face furled in concentration, a strip of white skin at the hairline telling her he wore a hat outdoors. And when he turned those auburn eyes on her, Tasia wondered how she'd ever objected to such a striking man's presence in their home.

"Doctor Kutsenko," said Eleni. "Please meet my sister Anastasia."

"Call me, 'Tasia,' Doctor."

"Very glad to make your acquaintance." He bowed slightly. "Two such hospitable young ladies as landlords? How could I help but be pleased?"

"Doctor Kutsenko has just returned from quite a journey, Tasia," said Eleni.

"Oh?"

"Yes, six months on the Subcontinent." He said zestfully. "I was telling a few yarns in your parlor earlier, wasn't I, Eleni? Well, none I can't repeat to you Tasia, should we find the time."

Tasia found that she liked this educated, active and extremely good-looking man. She stepped from the shadows of the landing into the full light of the bedroom.

And Doctor Kutsenko frowned. "Are you twins? Eleni, you never mentioned..."

"Yes," said Tasia, feeling sheepish. "We are."

"But not identical. Eleni is a little taller, and your faces aren't quite the same—though both pretty, I should say."

"Whose is prettiest?" asked Eleni with an over-broad smile.

"Impossible to judge. It's like choosing between *Venus with a Mirror* and Melzi's *Flora* in the Hermitage. As soon as you pick one, the other calls your heart."

"Doctor, do you always flirt so with twenty-year-old landladies?"

"You misunderstand me, Anastasia. My interest is purely academic." He shook his finger as if to pretend to scold her. "Twins, you see, fascinate me scientifically. Identicals are best, of course, for long-term biological study, but fraternals have their value too." He pressed his fingertips together below his chin. "My eyes show me that you are similar. Now, if you will humor me, let your voices say how you are different."

The sisters stood in thoughtful silence for several moments to this strange questioning before Eleni, with a shrug, said "Tasia can't cook."

"And Eleni *won't* cook," laughed Tasia. "She's lazy."

"I'll cook for polite people. I'll cook for *him!*"

"Ladies," Doctor Kutsenko said with a chuckle. "You show me your differences are far more than cooking."

Eleni laughed and Tasia was about to join in when the edge of her eye caught motion somewhere in or around a trunk near the window.

Tasia blinked, unsure what she had seen. Nothing moved again, if it ever had. It was quite an odd trunk, really, large and perfectly cubical. A sail-like cloth was pulled tightly over its form. And was that the impression of bars beneath?

"Doctor Kutsenko, please pardon me for asking, but what is that...that structure underneath the tarp? A cage?"

"Yes. My specimen cage." He said without emotion. "Besides being a medical doctor and surgeon, I take interest in biological diversity in all its myriad forms. I regularly contribute to zoos and university collections throughout Europe." He sat back against the dresser, his hip disrupting the neatly aligned scalpels. "On this journey, though, I failed to gather anything of interest. The cage lies empty." He seemed to steel himself against the disappointment. "Much to the dismay of my backers, I should say. Still—*Tut! Tut!*—there are other ways to make money, aren't there?"

"I thought I saw movement inside."

"The bedroom window is open and the breeze simply ruffles the cover."

"Oh."

"I helped him carry it in here," whispered Eleni. "It's too light I think to be anything but empty."

Tasia nodded.

After a pause, Doctor Kutsenko said "Well, I really should return to my unpacking. As you raised the subject of cooking, Eleni, I'll remind you to please serve my dinners before four o'clock. Any later and I have the most ghastly nightmares. A temperamental condition I've been cursed with since a child."

"Anything you wish, Doctor."

"And I'll mention to you, Tasia, incase your sister hasn't, that I intend to resume my medical practice now that I've returned to Odessa. As a surgeon, I may have callers at ungodly hours. I hope the sum I'm paying for this room offsets the inconvenience of a few bleary eyes. Can I depend on you and your sister to lend some small assistance when needed?"

"Of course, Doctor Kutsenko," said Tasia. "We would find it most interesting."

"Wonderful. We're all going to be great friends."

As they left the bedroom for the landing, he muttered: "Twins—such possibilities."

A step down the stairs, Eleni whispered: "Did you hear him, Tasia? He said we had possibilities."

"Possibilities for biological study."

"Marriage is a form of biological study, isn't it?"

"You've been reading those ladies' journals at the English Club, Eleni." Though Tasia couldn't help but wonder who the doctor might prefer... "He does seem very nice. But what do you think about that cage? Are you sure it's empty?"

"Not, absolutely certain of course. That cloth covers all of it, and it's fastened tight as a drum at the base. But, even so large, it was a feather when we carried it. It had to be empty."

"My mistake, I suppose."

They descended the last steps into the parlor. Tasia went to her market basket on the table and withdrew the newspaper she'd bought.

The war with Japan dominated the front page, but when she turned to the second, Tasia saw the inside headline:

ROSE THIEF STRIKES AGAIN

"Another robbery," she muttered.

"Where was this one?" asked Eleni, coming up behind to read over her shoulder.

Tasia read aloud: "A trio of Repin masterwork paintings were stolen Saturday night from the Vorontsov Palace, three playing cards left in their places. Police believe the thief may be a foreigner, as the cards, which substitute the suit of diamonds with roses, are of Ottoman origin."

"Foreigner?" scoffed Tasia. "Anyone can buy those cards at the Privoz bazaar for a kopeck a pack. And they're Persian not Ottoman."

"That article's slander. It doesn't mention anything about the charitable things the Rose has done. Leaving bundles of money—and those cards, again, old news here—at orphanages, churches, hospitals..."

"A pittance compared to what he's stolen, Eleni."

"He gives to those who need it. Like that famous English thief. 'Something...Hood,' wasn't it?"

Tasia tried to recall what she'd read in the London papers from the English Club. "'Hook,' I think it was."

"That's it!" Eleni snapped her fingers. "Hook! *Captain* Hook."

"Yes," said Tasia flipping the newspaper page. "Well, let's hope your Captain Hook leaves a little money around here. We could use some good luck..."

Sometime past four in the morning an exhausted Tasia opened their front door. A man outside in a hooded cape stepped forward, the cowl pulled so low she could only see his thin lips and stubbly chin. With a metallic scent in his breath he said:

"Is Doctor Dikopavlenko here?"

"Dikopavlenko?" repeated Eleni, standing behind Tasia, a kitchen knife hidden in her robes. "Who's he?"

"We've a Doctor Kutsenko." said Tasia firmly. "Is that who you want?"

"That'll do." The man lurched hard against the door, knocking Tasia from the threshold, and forcing himself into the house. Both women shouted, and Eleni readied the knife, yet the effort of barging inside sapped this stranger of his strength. He toppled forward, Tasia barely able to catch him before he hit the floor.

"Eleni," she said, straining to keep the big man up. "Help me."

Eleni pocketed her knife and slipped an arm under his shoulder. They both shouted for the doctor.

He was already on the stairwell. "Take him up to my room."

"He's bleeding," said Eleni.

She was right. Red droplets were falling from inside the hood, some landing on Tasia's bare feet as they hauled him across the parlor. Doctor Kutsenko joined them at the stairs, hoisting the man up, half across his shoulders as they climbed the steps. Eleni had an arm, and Tasia a leg but it was like carrying nothing. The Doctor ably shouldered the load alone.

When they reached Kutsenko's room, they set the wounded man down on the bed, propped his head upon a stack of pillows. The doctor pushed back the hood.

Eleni, not at all squeamish, let out a breath.

The remnant of a wine bottle protruded from his opened skull, the cylindrical shard lodged just above the cheekbone and encompassing all the right eye socket. Dried blood covered his face and neck, new crimson seeping over the pillows.

"Doctor..." said the man, his one visible eye cloudy and

distant. "I..."

"Artur Kutsenko," replied their tenant.

"I can't pull it out. Something's hooked in there, Doc."

The doctor patted the man on the shoulder, then moved to the dresser to select his instruments. He silently shuffled through them for a moment, lifting a wiry hook and something resembling rose prunes, before he glanced at the girls:

"Eleni, Tasia, please close the door on your way out. This is no scene for young ladies."

◎　◎　◎

"You saved his life."

"I can't say that for certain, Tasia. Only that procedure went better than expected."

"How could a man in such dire condition walk out of here so alert and seemingly in good spirits a day or so later?" Standing in Doctor Kutsenko's airy, morning bedroom, Tasia folded up the stained sheets on which the patient had lain for two days before leaving. "Doctor, you are a miracle worker."

"Hardly. What I did most competent surgeons could have done if they applied themselves." His voice turned gruff. "It's only that they *won't.*"

She looked at him curiously, folded the last sheet.

"You see, Tasia, this twentieth century we've entered has no limitations scientific or otherwise. Daring medical practitioners –those outside the conservative schools of the establishment–can mend tissues, cure ills our forbearers never dreamed possible. We are not far, I think, from keeping the Reaper at bay forever. A worthy man, if properly maintained by his lessers, may live indefinitely. Are you open-minded, Tasia?"

"I think so."

"Let us see." He began to unbutton his shirt.

"Doctor Kutsenko!"

He laughed. "Nothing of that sort, Tasia. Observe..." Turning away from her, he pulled out the tails of his shirt, then hoisted it up to his shoulders. In the center of his back, on either side of his spine, were two thick oval scars. "I live on the kidneys of another man. Two in fact."

She'd never heard of such things. "Is that possible?"

"If it weren't, I wouldn't be standing before you now." He let the shirt down, turned back to her. "A surgeon living along a remote tributary of the Ganges performed the first operation, the second was in Peking by a soon-to-be-murdered physician loyal to Prince Qing. Great men, great methods chased into the shadows even in their own nations by centuries of imperialism. I learned the methods from my benefactors. Now, I return the favor to those in need."

It seemed something out of Verne or Wells. "Are there any drawbacks?"

"Only moral. But if it saves lives..."

"Then it's worth it."

"Yes. We are similar, aren't we, Tasia? You can inform Eleni, if you wish, but please keep this conversation within the household. The closed-minded, you see...I won't let men die, Tasia, waiting for some committee of medical bureaucrats to say what I do is permissible. I'd rather take the risk, than lose the great man."

So brave... "You're not a criminal, Doctor Kutsenko. You're an angel."

"Well, some might say. But angels have wings on their backs, not scars." He tucked in his shirttails. "Anyway, it's well past time you called me 'Artur.'"

"Artur."

"And it's you, Tasia, who may yet see the angels. Angels in the architecture along Yekaterininskaya Street that is. I invite you for a city-center stroll and fine dining tomorrow night. Unencumbered by your sister, of course."

This surprised Tasia, nervous butterflies fluttering about her stomach. "I think such...such...meetings with our male lodgers are against the rules, Artur."

"Oh. You are certain then?" His disappointment was palpable, more than a hint of offense in his tone.

Tasia felt a silly girl. She was twenty after all, without any serious suitors. What had he said? *I'd rather take the risk than lose the great man...*

Stop being such a prude, Tasia.

"Of course, as you say, Artur, rules are made to be broken. Mother might never know."

Tasia flipped another page in *Tess of the d'Urbervilles.*

"Where have you been all night?"

Eleni tossed her umbrella in the door basket, stripped off her raincoat. "The Medical College Library."

"To nearly ten o'clock?"

"I've been checking surgeons' registries." She hung the coat on the wall peg. "There's no listing for a Doctor Kutsenko in Odessa or the whole oblast."

"He never claimed to be a *registered* surgeon."

Eleni pushed over a footstool, then sat down on the divan next to Tasia. "But there *was* a listing for a Doctor Isa Alexandervich Dikopavlenko, Practicing Surgeon, in three consecutive volumes. Until he was expelled by the Medical Council in December 1900."

"Why?"

"The registry didn't say."

Tasia shut her book. "Artur's a good tenant, Eleni. Why are you suddenly so skeptical of him? You saw him save that man with a bottle through his eye."

"I did. A man who called him 'Dikopavlenko.'"

"A man with a head injury. He might have called Artur anything in such a state."

"Including his actual name. I don't trust a doctor living under an alias. How many tragedies have we suffered because of lodgers with false identities?"

"Are you sure, Eleni, this change of heart regarding Artur isn't merely jealousy? A bit of envy because a handsome surgeon asked me to dinner tomorrow night instead of you?"

"You know that's not true."

"I wonder. One of our tenants has shown interest in me, for once, and now you—"

It was more a bleating than a scream, like the cries of some dying animal echoing up from the Feliski slaughter yards. In an instant, both sisters were sprinting up the stairs to the second floor. The cries came from their tenant's room.

"Doctor Kutsenko," shouted Eleni, pounding on the door. "What is happening in there?"

There was a rustle inside, then something like the clinking of metal on glass. The metallic sound repeated, and the screams —whatever they were—subsided. Heavy footsteps followed, then Doctor Kutsenko tore open the door. He stood in his robe, hair disheveled, face night swollen.

"Artur," said Tasia. "Is everything all right?"

"Nightmares!" He half-screamed. "Eleni, why did you tempt me with the chocolate mousse past six? You know I can't have food at night."

"You ate it well enough."

"Well, I'm sorry for the screams. It was a manifold vision even Goya could not slumber through. I should think that I shall not disturb you any more tonight though. I've taken a sedative." He began to shut the door.

"Isa Alexandervich!" shouted Eleni.

He paused. "Why do you call me 'Isa'?"

"To see what you would do."

There came a knocking from downstairs.

"The front door," said Tasia. "At nearly ten..."

"Another emergency, perhaps," said the doctor wearily. He locked his own door, and the three of them descended the stairs together. When Tasia opened the front door, the same man in the hooded cape was on their step, his eyes clear and stern. Tasia noticed for the first time he had *heterochromia,* one iris blue, the other, the one in the socket where the bottle had been and now encircled by a ring of Doctor Kutzenko's stitches, was dark brown.

"Doctor," he said. "Your assistance is required."

The doctor nodded—and it seemed to Tasia that some

unspoken communication passed between the two men. Their tenant returned to his room. In moments, he was back down the stairs, dressed in a tan waistcoat, medical kit in hand. "I've disturbed you enough tonight. Please don't wait up, ladies."

"As if we would, Isa," said Eleni.

Tasia watched from the door as the pair climbed into a horse drawn buggy and sped away into Odessa's night.

◎　◎　◎

"It's nearly eight o'clock, Artur," said Tasia looking through the menu at elegant Fanconi's Café in the city center. "You'll eat too late..."

He laughed at this, glancing up from his own menu with those mesmerizing eyes. "I'll risk a few nightmares for a scrumptious meal at last, Tasia. Not that your sister's cooking isn't enjoyable, but..."

"No apologies. No one eats Eleni's dishes. I've lost so much weight since Mother's been gone...This dress hardly fits me..."

"Well, I think you look elegant." He said, and his gaze lingered on her figure.

"Thank you." Tasia felt herself blushing at the compliment and wondered if he could tell. To be out, free and un-chaperoned with a man like Artur at Falconi's, the legendary "hanging gardens" restaurant where the tycoons and nobility of the Russian Empire dined. Simple ethnic Greek girls of Tasia's class never ate here. She probably couldn't even merit work at Falconi's as a dishwasher...and these prices...

"Artur...our meal will cost three weeks rent. With the war, food is so expensive, it is not fair to you...'

"I have the means, Tasia. Enjoy yourself."

She nodded. Yet, his answer begged another question. One that perhaps should not be asked but the wine in the park before dinner had made Tasia brave and improper: "If you've monies available, Artur, then why do you stay at so simple a place as ours? Why not a fancy hotel? Or purchase a home?"

He frowned, a firmness in his response that made Tasia

regret her question. "Isn't it evident? My work demands a residency off the 'society' path. At least until the medical boards de-criminalize my methods." He took a long drink of his merlot and it seemed to Tasia his hand gripped the wine glass very tightly. "Every year I make overtures, always I am rejected. Idiots! How many Russian elite will die in this conflict with Japan whom I might have saved? If my techniques were applied these brave officers would still breathe."

"Only officers? Surely all soldiers could benefit?"

"Of course, of course," he drank more wine, "the heroic deserve to keep what is born theirs. But the supply must come from somewhere, Tasia. The common soldier will lay down his life on the battlefield for his commander. Is it much different to make that same sacrifice in a hospital bed? We'd win this war if men like Admiral Vitgeft had been given another spleen."

Tasia wondered if she was misunderstanding these rather curious words. "These skills of yours Artur, do many others have them?"

"No white man does. I can say that for certain. The Swiss and French, leaders here, can only stew in their juices with envy. Racists! Jingoists! They fail to look East. The Chinese surgeon Bian Que was performing organ replacement centuries before Christ's birth as was the great Indian physician Suśruta. The chaos of imperialism has pushed the knowledge to the corners of their societies, to hidden schools in lost grottos and Himalayan valleys seldom trod by Europeans. But they can be found by an intrepid scholar-adventurer who dares—and I am the one who has done so. When they told me my kidneys were failing I sought legendary places. If I live by a transplant, others here can too."

"And Odessa is very glad you're alive. As am I."

He did not smile. "Well, Odessa will be. Soon. That I guarantee you. If we..."

His words were interrupted by a looming presence within the restaurant. The head waiter lead a tall, serious-looking police constable past them to a fine-tailored elderly gentleman alone at the next table.

"You are Baron Kurakin? Owner of the Osmanov Warehouses?" asked the waiter.

"What is it?" replied the old man sternly, as if the waiter should know to whom he spoke. "Why do you interrupt my soup?"

"I'm sorry, sir," said the constable stepping forward, a tremor in his voice despite his towering size. "But there is a problem at your warehouse property. Our men have cornered the Rose Thief and his gang. We are breaking down the doors."

"At last," said the baron. "We'll kill that rogue, yet."

Arm-in-arm, Tasia and Artur walked above the seaside along Nikolaevsky Boulevard, a perfectly paved street skirting the edge of the Odessan Plateau: the gilded roofs and wrought-iron gates of palaces and mansions to their left, a viewing wall overlooking the harbor on the right. And, far above the branches of the white acacias lining the roadside, floated oriental lanterns launched from one of Odessa's many great plazas ahead. They lit up the April night sky, a manmade constellation of glowing orange orbs flying over the city, slowly being carried away by the winds to cast their lights on the dark waters of the Black Sea.

Tasia had never seen a more beautiful night.

Yet her escort possessed a different view. "All these Oriental lamps," said Artur looking high into the heavens, "it is an ill omen for this struggle with Japan. We will lose this war..."

Tasia patted his arm. "They are Chinese lanterns, not Japanese, take them as signs your work will be accepted..."

"What a pleasant interpretation. You are a remarkable woman, Anastasia Karadopoulina."

"Hardly."

He kissed her—a moment before she knew he would.

"Artur...we are unchaperoned."

"This is what unchaperoned people do, Tasia. Have you never been alone with a man?"

She pushed him away gently, unsure if she wished to. "People will see us."

"Maybe, another kiss when we are home?"

"Eleni will be there."

"You can't hide behind a sister forever. Is she as chaste with her sweethearts as you?"

"You and I mustn't be in the same house, Artur. If you wish to court me, you might find other lodgings."

"I'll do so, Monday morning."

"It's best."

They walked, silently holding hands for a few minutes. Tasia unsure of her own intentions. He was handsome, and a healer, but some of his recent words unsettled her. She'd ask Eleni. Jealousy aside her sister was always truthful. Blunt and tactless but truthful.

After several minutes, the Chinese lanterns fading to mere pinpoints over the sea, they passed into a plaza with the great neo-classical statue of Duke de Richelieu, and Odessa's famous Boulevard Staircase descending forever down to the harbor. At the top of these mighty steps, a portly police constable stood watch.

"Is it over?" Asked Artur as they passed through the plaza. "Did they catch the Rose at last?"

The constable shook his head. "Word is, he slipped away once again, sir, curse 'em. Twenty men with that devil at bay and still he escaped. We took a few of his men though."

"You'll never finish him. Not with our best off at war. And oafs like you left to mind the house."

"Well, never mind the war, sir. We aren't so incompetent as you say. There was blood on the road stones afterwards, some of our bullets found their marks. It didn't drop the devil, but it may take the bloom off the ole Rose, yet."

"I'll keep my wager on the great man."

"As you wish, sir."

After they'd exited the plaza, leaving the offended constable far behind, Tasia asked: "You admire the Rose Thief, don't you, Artur?"

"I admire his willingness to go outside the law for what is right, what is needed." His voice dropped to a whisper then, his words so low Tasia wondered if she was supposed to hear what was said next.

"And I understand his obsessions. God help me."

When they returned home, they found the front door ajar and the lodging house empty.

"Eleni!" shouted Tasia.

But there was no answer.

"It's unlike her to leave the premises unlocked," continued Tasia, checking the back courtyard for her sister.

"My door is open as well," said Artur peering up the stairs to the landing above. "Someone's been in my room."

"Eleni would never invade a tenant's privacy."

"The evidence would suggest otherwise, Tasia," he said tersely and began to ascend the stairs, when something stopped him.

A man appeared in the the front doorway.

"Doctor Dikopavlenko!" shouted this visitor. Tasia half-expected it would be the familiar hooded patient. Instead, this new caller was stockier, slightly older, dressed in a long black coat and red bowler hat. "We need your help!"

Artur stepped back, down to the parlor. "What help?"

The man stared at Tasia, "Is the lady...?"

"She's with me," said the doctor. "Speak freely."

"They shot the boss through the liver, Doc. He don't have long, lest you can do something. Can you come with me?"

"I'll get my surgeon's tools. I'll need your help to take everything. It's none too heavy. I've only one left."

The man in the bowler grunted an affirmative and the two climbed the stairs to Artur's room, Tasia trailing behind. There followed a whirlwind of activity as the doctor collected his blades, saws, and medicine bottles from the drawers and dresser tops, only pausing when he remarked about missing a scalpel.

"Doc, we got no time," said the other man. "The boss is half in his grave as is."

With his satchel pinned beneath one arm, Artur and this

visitor lifted the cage from the floor, hefting it past Tasia as they went from the bedroom to the landing.

It seemed to her something moved within. An inkling, an irrational suspicion, came to her then that somehow equated the motion inside with her missing sister. It made no sense, yet, Tasia still found herself reaching out a hand to lift the tarp's edge.

Artur slapped it away.

"We've no time for that, Tasia! A man is dying."

"What's in there, Artur?"

"Later!"

This resistance only increased her fears. They were halfway down the stairs, Artur first, bearing most of the weight of the cage when Tasia gritted her teeth and grabbed at the covering again.

The man in the bowler struck her hard in the jaw with his elbow. Tasia, lost her balance, slid down the few remaining steps to the parlor's floor, more stunned than injured. The men sped by her, carrying the cage through the room and out the front door.

"I'm sorry, Tasia. That was uncalled for," said Artur as they stepped into the street. "He'll live to regret that. I assure you as a gentleman."

Through the opened doorway, she could see them slide the cage into the back of a black horse-drawn van. The two men shut the rear door, then went around to climb into the seats at front.

Her wits returning, Tasia rushed to her feet, reached the doorway. The van was just pulling out into the night.

"I'll explain everything, Tasia, soon," shouted Artur from passenger seat. "You'll forgive me, I know. If you're a woman worthy of love, then you'll forgive. But, now, a brave man is at risk."

As the van distanced itself, that cage moved again, independent of the shuddering of the carriage over the street stones. She knew then. Knew whom that cage contained.

"Eleni!" Tasia sprung from the front step and sprinted after the van. "Eleni!"

"I'm here!" came a shout behind. Tasia turned around to see her sister and three police constables running up the street towards her.

The sisters embraced, Tasia whispering "Thank God, thank God."

"Where's Doctor Kutsenko? Where is that cage, Tasia?"

She pointed up the road.

"Is the cage empty?"

"No."

A moment later the constables were lost in the gloom of night, last seen in a vain pursuit of the van. The sisters returned to their home.

Under the lamplight of the parlor, Tasia could see Eleni looked impossibly tired, lines in her forehead, shadows beneath her eyes. She appeared ten years older than she had this afternoon. Though her own jaw stung, and was quickly swelling, Tasia felt the need to comfort her sister. But Eleni wanted nothing—no tea, no food, no blanket. Only to sit on that parlor chair, head in hands, and recover her strength.

"Tell me what happened," Tasia finally said softly.

"Don't you know?"

"How could I?"

Eleni lifted her face, eyes red and puffy. "Then you didn't see? You haven't seen?"

"I've seen nothing."

Tapping some new well of strength, Eleni moved her chair closer, leaning a shoulder against Tasia, as if she needed physical support to tell of her tale. Finally, she told her story in the hoarse, cracking voice of a much older woman.

ELENI'S ENCOUNTER

"I had been alone some hours this evening when I heard those familiar cries coming from our tenant's room. The long shrill bleating sounds he says he makes in his sleep when the nightmares come. But Doctor Kutsenko was away—out courting you, Tasia. Who or what then was up there? I listened to those shrill screeches for only a few seconds before I seized the spare key from the cabinet, and with lighted candlestick in hand, climbed the steps to the landing before the doctor's room. Only then did I pause, Tasia. The noise was horrifying, like a despondent creature awaiting the fall of a butcher's axe. It took all my will to slip the key into the lock and turn the bolt. As I opened the door, the cries went silent. Whatever made those noises was aware of me, knew I was inside the room with it. After those incessant shrieks, the quiet itself somehow became frightening.

At first glance, the bedroom appeared undisturbed, exactly as it had been when Doctor Kutsenko was present. I used the candlestick to light the chamber lamps. The doctor's wardrobe was open, few clothes hung inside, and I could see that nothing of any size dwelt there. Of course, my attention went to that covered cage by the window. As I grew closer, and the boards creaked beneath my feet, an impression appeared underneath the tarp, as if a hand, or perhaps a face, were pressed against the fabric trying to peer through. It quickly faded. I stared for several moments but the face—if had been a face—did not return. Still, I pulled one of Doctor Kutsenko's scalpels from the top of his dresser and kept it ready as I approached the cage. Gripping the pen's corner at a full arm's length, I shook it slightly, then harder. Nothing moved underneath, though it seemed weighted down, heavier than when I'd helped the doctor carry it in a week ago."

Tasia brushed her sister's hair with her fingers, feeling the perspiration, the warmth of great emotion on her skin. "I observed him carrying the cage tonight, Eleni. Artur has a way of bearing all the weight. It might seem light to you no matter the contents."

"Could be. Could be, Tasia. All I knew at that moment alone up there was that the cage was too heavy *now* to be empty. Keeping the scalpel ready, I hiked up the end of tarp nearest me. What I saw inside drove waves of revulsion through me...sick, primal emotions that sent me scampering back a few steps. They didn't last, Tasia. Thank God. As I recovered, a terrible pity took my soul. It was a boy inside, maybe fifteen or sixteen, emaciated, wearing only a loincloth. I couldn't tell his race or ethnicity, I could see little of his features for he was huddled at the other end of the pen back to me. His face in profile, peering over his own shoulder, I could see but one terribly-pained intelligent dark eye staring back at me. Oh, the poor creature. On the boy's back ran a thin, oval scar outlining where his left kidney must be. Or must have been. His bare skin too was pockmarked by countless needle scars, he must have spent this last week, or much longer, drugged into delirium. The boy was the saddest sight I've ever seen. And there were signs, Tasia, hints that the cage's population wasn't always so sparse. That perhaps two or even three souls might have occupied it recently. I didn't attempt to communicate with the prisoner, I wasn't thinking then. I knew only that I wished to free him. I quickly found a set of keys in the drawer of the wardrobe, trying the members until I discovered one that fit. I opened the padlock, pushed the tarp higher, and pulled open that door. The captive stirred at the motion, turning towards me, tentatively at first, but faster as he gained resolve. As he did so, more of his form became visible. His chest and stomach were covered in those damnable uniform, deliberate scars. Scars made not by some terrible accident, but by the precision of a surgeon's knife. He had prominent mark at his throat, but the most gruesome lay at the face. His other eye, the one initially hidden by his posture, was missing. Instead, the eyelid over the socket was pulled tight and flat, a fresh suture along the upper cheek holding it in place forever. No bulge of any eyeball remained beneath. It had been removed, Tasia. All these horrors I grasped for but a moment. The boy crawled forward to the opening, face nearly in mine, and tried to speak. But only the hideous bleat erupted from his lips. It was no foreign language, something had been taken. His speech stolen from him.

"I lost my composure then, Tasia. I dropped the scalpel, it fell beside the cage, but, I failed to retrieve it. Instead, I tugged down the tarp, blocked the sight of him, fled out the room and down the stairs as those blaring bleating cries erupted from behind. It was a cowardly act, I admit. By the time, I reached the parlor I'd regained *some* of my senses. That creature, that poor boy out of a Mary Shelley nightmare, was not the monster. He was a victim. Doctor Kutsenko was the true monster. And then I thought of you. That devil Kutsenko was somewhere in this city with my sister. I panicked then. I didn't know what he might do to you out there, Tasia. He might have a dozen flats, a dozen cages... I fled the house searching for a policeman. When I returned, you were here, and I'm grateful to Mary, Jesus and Saint Symeon that you are. But that tragic child... Why would he cut him up like that?"

"He's a harvestman, Eleni. But if I told you what that fiend was harvesting you'd never believe me. The possibilities–and the horrors–of the twentieth century are endless."

She looked at me. And she knew.

◉　◉　◉

The police found the van less than an hour later. It was off on a side street near Frantsusky Boulevard, the horses standing calm, the carriage quiet, the rear door ajar. The driver, his red bowler floating in a pool of crimson on the floor, had fallen onto the leads when he died, pulling the reins tight and slowing the obedient stallions to a standstill. His throat, like Doctor Kutsenko's next to him, had been slit from behind by 'a precise instrument well-suited for the task.' The police suspected the weapon was one of the surgeon's own scalpels. In the van, a cage was found empty with the door open, the remnants of a shredded tarp nearby inside.

The murderer of Doctor Kutsenko and his associate has never been found.

WATERPROOF

MARCELINA VIZCARRA

As the train pulled into Waterproof, mothers swept their children indoors, shutters slammed and locked, the sheriff pulled his wife's brother, the town drunk, across the porch of the jail and inside to safety. The painted ladies at the Calliope, who knew a little something about temptation, peeked between the curtains at the couple holding hands at the depot. Newlyweds. Of course, they were in a hurry.

The steam whistle drowned the sounds of the fight at the apothecary where Tom Beadle chased his son, Junebug, into the street and yanked the bindle from the boy's hands. The nearby tourists watched with relish, as if happening upon a silent film in real life, as the pair mouthed oaths at each other, one's arms flapping in frustrated flight, the other's legs kicking underwear and tooth powder out of reach. Junebug gathered his belongings and stumbled onto the train platform.

Tom couldn't believe his son could be this naïve. Changing

time-climates on a whim. Nobody in Waterproof rushed anything. Even elections and executions often stalled until worthier candidates were found. Now, the wheezing train needed only to catch its breath before stealing Junebug away. "Work another year," Tom said. "Save some more money before you leave. Then, if you still want to go, I'll match you dollar for dollar."

"Thanks, but no thanks, Pa. I'm stagnating here."

Stella had said the same thing when she handed over Junebug at the depot seventeen years ago. Tom blamed her for their son's wanderlust—and himself too—since the boy had been conceived during that peculiar ambition of courtship, when everything resembles an escape-hatch from boredom. Boredom meaning the shackles of reality.

Even then, the chronodrought had already lasted decades, had already made people bolt for the coasts: the north, the east, where time precipitated, dense as water. But after Junebug was born, Tom changed his mind. As Stella boarded the train, he recited the jetlag of childhood milestones, hoping she might stay. She simply faced the horizon, as though she couldn't hear him over the thunder of her thoughts.

"The weather will surprise you," Tom said now. "The almanac predicts a monsoon in New York." Junebug's eyes gleamed. Tom instantly realized his mistake. No doubt the towered city was the boy's chosen destination. Tom's blame shifted toward the tourists, the retirees, and their Vernian tales of undersea travel and rockets to the moon like that Méliès film, *Le Voyage dans la Lune,* shown when Tom was a boy by a newcomer with a hand-cranked camera.

And hadn't Tom shown Junebug the same film when the newcomer traded it for laudanum? Hadn't he perpetuated the romance of escape? Waterproof was a prison, he might as well have said, a drying puddle where everyone makes constant concessions just to justify their optimism. Optimism meaning thirst.

Down the street, boxcars opened to allow the mechanical arm to hand out water barrels, rolled away to be rationed later by the deputies. The train panted like an animal stranded in the desert. A few moments more, and it'd lurch from its place in a bid for survival. "If you just stick around for a while, things will improve," Tom said, raking his tumbleweed of beard. He eyed the cartilaginous specimens hanging from the butcher's eaves, the dust-furred candy jars in his own apothecary window. "We have penicillin now. Didn't have that when I was a boy. And the new dentist that turned us off tinfoil fillings." Occasionally, a tourist left behind a music player, and the townsfolk gathered around it, listening to spongy snippets until the batteries gave out.

Junebug already had one foot on the car step, one hand on the grab bar. Through the windows, Tom caught the gaze of a tattooed woman drinking out of a plastic canteen, a man that looked as if he'd fallen face first into a notions box. He couldn't compete with such inducements. Tom slipped his father's watch into Junebug's hand.

"Don't worry, Pa," Junebug said, swinging up and into the vestibule. "I know what I'm doing."

"Hey, pal, where can I get a drink around here?" a tourist asked, cuffing at Tom's shoulder.

◉　◉　◉

Newcomers stumbled into the Calliope. The saloon's furniture was strewn topsy-turvy, as though arranged by flood. "Well, hello, hello, all you tin-toothed cowards. Still desiccating in your hundred-year-old drawers, I see," a polyester cowboy said. "I'm here to fetch my hat." He slapped the counter with the impatience typical of tourists. "Sarsaparilla," he said. "Haven't had one since I was a boy, the day I forgot this, in fact." The stranger snatched the child-sized hat from the lost-and-found box and balanced it atop his head.

"I found it this morning when I was sweeping," the bartender said.

"No kidding? Then you might as well throw out all this other junk," he said, pawing through the cravat pins and skeleton keys. The owners are probably daisy fertilizer by now." The newcomer turned his sunburned face to Tom. "You look familiar."

"I run the apothecary."

"That's it. You sold me a quart of lemon drops when I was a boy. Or should I say yesterday." He threw air-quotes over his head which Tom thought made him appear just as juvenile as the last time he'd seen him. "That junk made my face pucker to the size of my fist. Still, fresher than anything in the train's dining car. So, kudos on that. Ever been?"

Tom ignored him.

"I asked if you've ever ridden the train." He snapped his fingers in front of Tom's face. "Of course not. I forgot. You're the same age as me. If you ever left, you'd be dead before you got back." He let go a laugh that ended in a dry cough.

"Sorry to hear about Junebug leaving," the bartender said, handing Tom another bottle of bourbon.

"He was a good boy."

The stranger tsked into his mug. "You let your son leave town without you?" The newcomer made a show of looking at his wristwatch, a piece that estimated time for six major cities. "Your grandchildren are probably graduating from college about now. What a pity you rubes are so afraid of the weather."

Tom started to protest, but some fool started hammering on the steam organ. The newcomer had already drifted into another conversation.

Tom paid the bartender and slouched outside into the static of dusk. Passing the jail, he heard the sheriff and his brother-in-law laughing over a game of cards. He saw the tracks swerving east into darkness, could just make out the husks of dwellings abandoned when the lightning veered too close. One morning, the sheriff had found Jamison's boy out there, skin sucked into the bone cavities, eyes as black as anthracite. Hear tell, the room had melted around him into a vitreous puddle.

◎　◎　◎

In the apartment above the apothecary, Tom stumbled around the chairs and their ghostly doubles as he packed his clothes, his razor, the single postcard Stella sent from New

Orleans—a naked woman wearing a mask on the front, indecipherable blotches on the back. When Stella's body returned, draped with a sheet, Tom refused to look underneath. She'd arrived only two days after she left. While Tom concocted infant formula at the apothecary counter, she'd cavorted in parades, he imagined, riding in the oared rocket from the Méliès film.

What had he missed by staying in this godforsaken town, this island of desert? He pictured a lifeboat slipping past, full of doppelgangers lofting trophies and moneybags, rocking women on their laps.

His father had ridden out one clear morning and returned hours later, withered, repentant. He made Tom promise to work the apothecary, to keep his life as small and still as the dioramas Jamison sold to the tourists.

Before Tom locked his shop, he pocketed a daguerreotype of Junebug swinging on a cardboard moon. He'd deliver the photograph, that was all, because the boy had forgotten it in his haste.

◎   ◎   ◎

As Tom waited on the platform, the newcomer strolled over, tipped his undersized hat at Tom. "Proving me wrong, are you?" he asked. Tom raised his chin.

Tom suspected it'd hurt to accelerate, his body distorting like rubber, or splitting like the mercury beads he'd chased with his pestle. Either one would be worth it if he could locate Junebug. A task, Tom reckoned, that would approximate jumping into a cyclone.

The express sped into Waterproof. Somebody got off the forward car. Tom boarded with the newcomer. The refrigerated air felt clammy against his skin. The gas of hygiene chemicals made his eyes water. He tried to ignore the women wearing men's undershirts. Once seated, he noticed his reflection in the window. He looked old, tired. He was both. He didn't recall shaving this morning, though maybe he was too drunk to remember. He lifted his hand to his beard. No, he hadn't shaved.

From the other side of the glass, the reflection motioned to him, stepped forward. As Tom watched, the reflection dangled his father's watch at the end of a broken fob, then abruptly slid sideways as the train jerked forward. Tom called to Junebug to wait and shoved past the newcomer, still battling his valise in the aisle. The train was out of town before Tom reached the vestibule. He gripped the bar and shut his eyes. Even through his eyelids, he could see the lightning, snapping like ropes against the horizon.

THE TRAVELER'S STORY OF A TERRIBLY STRANGE BED

WILKIE COLLINS

Shortly after my education at college was finished, I happened to be staying at Paris with an English friend. We were both young men then, and lived, I am afraid, rather a wild life, in the delightful city of our sojourn. One night we were idling about the neighbourhood of the Palais Royal, doubtful to what amusement we should next betake ourselves. My friend proposed a visit to Frascati's; but his suggestion was not to my taste. I knew Frascati's, as the French saying is, by heart; had lost and won plenty of five-franc pieces there, merely for amusement's sake, until it was amusement no longer, and was thoroughly tired, in fact, of all the ghastly respectabilities of such a social anomaly as a respectable gambling-house.

"For Heaven's sake," said I to my friend, "let us go somewhere where we can see a little genuine, blackguard, poverty-stricken gaming, with no false gingerbread glitter thrown over it at all. Let us get away from fashionable Frascati's, to a house where they don't mind letting in a man with a ragged coat, or a man with no coat, ragged or otherwise."

"Very well," said my friend, "we needn't go out of the Palais Royal to find the sort of company you want. Here's the place just before us; as blackguard a place, by all report, as you could possibly wish to see." In another minute we arrived at the door, and entered the house.

When we got up stairs, and had left our hats and sticks with the doorkeeper, we were admitted into the chief gambling room. We did not find many people assembled there. But, few as the men were who looked up at us on our entrance, they were all types–lamentably true types–of their respective classes.

We had come to see blackguards; but these men were something worse. There is a comic side, more or less appreciable, in all blackguardism–here there was nothing but tragedy–mute, weird tragedy. The quiet in the room was horrible. The thin, haggard, long-haired young man, whose sunken eyes fiercely watched the turning up of the cards, never spoke; the flabby, fat-faced, pimply player, who pricked his piece of pasteboard perseveringly, to register how often black won, and how often red–never spoke; the dirty, wrinkled old man, with the vulture eyes and the darned greatcoat, who had lost his last *sou,* and still looked on desperately, after he could play no longer–never spoke. Even the voice of the croupier sounded as if it were strangely dulled and thickened in the atmosphere of the room. I had entered the place to laugh; but the spectacle before me was something to weep over. I soon found it necessary to take refuge in excitement from the depression of spirits which was fast stealing on me. Unfortunately I sought the nearest excitement, by going to the table, and beginning to play. Still more unfortunately, as the event will show, I won–won prodigiously; won incredibly; won at such a rate, that the regular players at the table crowded round me; and staring at my stakes with hungry, superstitious eyes, whispered to one another, that the English stranger was going to break the bank.

The game was *Rouge et Noir.* I had played at it in every city in

Europe, without, however, the care or the wish to study the Theory of Chances—that philosopher's stone of all gamblers! And a gambler, in the strict sense of the word, I had never been. I was heart-whole from the corroding passion for play. My gaming was a mere idle amusement. I never resorted to it by necessity, because I never knew what it was to want money. I never practised it so incessantly as to lose more than I could afford, or to gain more than I could coolly pocket without being thrown off my balance by my good luck. In short, I had hitherto frequented gambling-tables—just as I frequented ballrooms and operahouses—because they amused me, and because I had nothing better to do with my leisure hours.

But on this occasion it was very different—now, for the first time in my life, I felt what the passion for play really was. My success first bewildered, and then, in the most literal meaning of the word, intoxicated me. Incredible as it may appear, it is nevertheless true, that I only lost when I attempted to estimate chances, and played according to previous calculation. If I left everything to luck, and staked without any care or consideration, I was sure to win—to win in the face of every recognised probability in favour of the bank. At first, some of the men present ventured their money safely enough on my colour; but I speedily increased my stakes to sums which they dared not risk. One after another they left off playing, and breathlessly looked on at my game.

Still, time after time, I staked higher and higher, and still won. The excitement in the room rose to fever pitch. The silence was interrupted by a deep, muttered chorus of oaths and exclamations in different languages, every time the gold was shovelled across to my side of the table—even the imperturbable croupier dashed his rake on the floor in a (French) fury of astonishment at my success. But one man present preserved his self-possession; and that man was my friend. He came to my side, and whispering in English, begged me to leave the place satisfied with what I had already gained. I must do him the justice to say, that he repeated his warnings and entreaties several times; and only left me and went away, after I had rejected his advice (I was to all intents and purposes gambling drunk) in terms which rendered it impossible for him to address me again that night.

Shortly after he had gone, a hoarse voice behind me cried: "Permit me, my dear sir! Permit me to restore to their proper place two Napoleons which you have dropped. Wonderful luck, sir! I pledge you my word of honour as an old soldier, in the course of my long experience in this sort of thing, I never saw such luck as yours!—Never! Go on, sir—*Sacre mille bombes!* Go on boldly, and break the bank!"

I turned round and saw, nodding and smiling at me with inveterate civility, a tall man, dressed in a frogged and braided surtout.

If I had been in my senses, I should have considered him, personally, as being rather a suspicious specimen of an old soldier. He had goggling bloodshot eyes, mangy mustachios, and a broken nose. His voice betrayed a barrack-room intonation of the worst order, and he had the dirtiest pair of hands I ever saw—even in France. These little personal peculiarities exercised, however, no repelling influence on me. In the mad excitement, the reckless triumph of that moment, I was ready to "fraternize" with anybody who encouraged me in my game. I accepted the old soldier's offered pinch of snuff; clapped him on the back, and swore he was the honestest fellow in the world—the most glorious relic of the Grand Army that I had ever met with. "Go on!" cried my military friend, snapping his fingers in ecstasy, "Go on, and win! Break the bank—*Mille tonnerres!* My gallant English comrade, break the bank!"

And I *did* go on—went on at such a rate, that in another quarter of an hour the croupier called out: "Gentlemen! the bank has discontinued for to-night." All the notes, and all the gold in that "bank," now lay in a heap under my hands; the whole floating capital of the gambling-house was waiting to pour into my pockets!

"Tie up the money in your pocket-handkerchief, my worthy sir," said the old soldier, as I wildly plunged my hands into my heap of gold. "Tie it up, as we used to tie up a bit of dinner in the Grand Army; your winnings are too heavy for any breeches pockets that ever were sewed. There! that's it!—shovel them in, notes and all! *Credie* what luck!—Stop! another Napoleon on the floor! *Ah! Mere petit polisson de Napoleon!* have I found thee at last? Now then, sir—two tight double knots each way with your honourable permission, and the money's safe. Feel it! feel it, fortunate sir! hard and round as a cannonball—*Ah, bah!* if they had only fired such cannon balls at us at Austerlitz—*nom d'une pipe!* if they only had! And now, as an ancient grenadier, as an ex-brave of the French army, what remains for me to do? I ask what? Simply this: to entreat my valued English friend to drink a bottle of champagne with me, and toast the goddess Fortune in foaming goblets before we part!"

Excellent ex-brave! Convivial ancient grenadier! Champagne by all means! An English cheer for an old soldier! Hurrah! Hurrah! Another English cheer for the goddess Fortune! Hurrah! Hurrah! Hurrah!

"Bravo! the Englishman; the amiable, gracious Englishman, in whose veins circulates the vivacious blood of France! Another glass? *Ah, bah!*—the bottle is empty! Nevermind! *Vive le vin!* I, the old soldier, order another bottle, and half a pound of *bon-bons* with it!"

"No, no, ex-brave; never—ancient grenadier! *Your* bottle last time; *my* bottle this. Behold it! Toast away! The French Army! —The great Napoleon! —The present company! The croupier! The honest croupier's wife and daughters—if he has any! The Ladies generally! Everybody in the world!"

By the time the second bottle of champagne was emptied, I felt as if I had been drinking liquid fire—my brain seemed all a-flame. No excess in wine had ever had this effect on me before in my life. Was it the result of a stimulant acting upon my system when I was in a highly excited state? Was my stomach in a particularly disordered condition? Or was the champagne amazingly strong?

"Ex-brave of the French Army!" cried I, in a mad state of

exhilaration, "*I* am on fire! How are *you?* You have set me on fire! Do you hear, my hero of Austerlitz? Let us have a third bottle of champagne to put the flame out!"

The old soldier wagged his head, rolled his goggle eyes, until I expected to see them slip out of their sockets; placed his dirty forefinger by the side of his broken nose; solemnly ejaculated "Coffee!" and immediately ran off into an inner room.

The word pronounced by the eccentric veteran seemed to have a magical effect on the rest of the company present. With one accord they all rose to depart. Probably they had expected to profit by my intoxication; but finding that my new friend was benevolently bent on preventing me from getting dead drunk, had now abandoned all hope of thriving pleasantly on my winnings. Whatever their motive might be, at any rate they went away in a body. When the old soldier returned, and sat down again opposite to me at the table, we had the room to ourselves. I could see the croupier, in a sort of vestibule which opened out of it, eating his supper in solitude. The silence was now deeper than ever.

A sudden change, too, had come over the 'ex-brave.' He assumed a portentously solemn look; and when he spoke to me again, his speech was ornamented by no oaths, enforced by no finger-snapping, enlivened by no apostrophes or exclamations.

"Listen, my dear sir," said he, in mysteriously confidential tones—"listen to an old soldier's advice. I have been to the mistress of the house (a very charming woman, with a genius for cookery!) to impress on her the necessity of making us some particularly strong and good coffee. You must drink this coffee in order to get rid of your little amiable exaltation of spirits before you think of going home—you *must*, my good and gracious friend! With all that money to take home tonight, it is a sacred duty to yourself to have your wits about you. You are known to be a winner to an enormous extent by several gentlemen present to-night, who, in a certain point of view, are very worthy and excellent fellows; but they are mortal men, my dear sir, and they have their amiable weaknesses! Need I say more? Ah, no, no! you understand me! Now, this is what you must do—send for a cabriolet when you feel quite well again—draw up all the windows when you get into it—and tell the driver to take you home only through the large and well lighted thoroughfares. Do this; and you and your money will be safe. Do this; and tomorrow you will thank an old soldier for giving you a word of honest advice."

Just as the ex-brave ended his oration in very lachrymose tones, the coffee came in, ready poured out in two cups. My attentive friend handed me one of the cups with a bow. I was parched with thirst, and drank it off at a draught. Almost instantly afterwards, I was seized with a fit of giddiness, and felt more completely intoxicated than ever. The room whirled round and round furiously; the old soldier seemed to be regularly bobbing up and down before me like the piston of a steam engine. I was half deafened by a violent singing in my ears; a feeling of utter bewilderment, helplessness, idiocy, overcame me. I rose from my chair, holding on by the table to keep my balance; and stammered out, that I felt dreadfully unwell—so unwell that I did not know how I was to get home.

"My dear friend," answered the old soldier, and even his voice seemed to be bobbing up and down as he spoke—"my dear friend, it would be madness to go home in *your* state; you would be sure to lose your money; you might be robbed and murdered with the greatest ease. *I* am going to sleep here: do *you* sleep here, too—they make up capital beds in this house—take one; sleep off the effects of the wine, and go home safely with your winnings to-morrow—to-morrow, in broad daylight."

I had but two ideas left: one, that I must never let go hold of my handkerchief full of money; the other, that I must lie down somewhere immediately, and fall off into a comfortable sleep. So I agreed to the proposal about the bed, and took the offered arm of the old soldier, carrying my money with my disengaged hand. Preceded by the croupier, we passed along some passages and up a flight of stairs into the bed-room which I was to occupy. The ex-brave shook me warmly by the hand; proposed that we should breakfast together, and then, followed by the croupier, left me for the night.

I ran to the wash-hand stand; drank some of the water in my jug; poured the rest out, and plunged my face into it—then sat down in a chair and tried to compose myself. I soon felt better. The change for my lungs, from the fetid atmosphere of the gambling-room to the cool air of the apartment I now occupied; the almost equally refreshing change for my eyes, from the glaring gas-lights of the "Salon" to the dim, quiet nicker of one bedroom candle; aided wonderfully the restorative effects of cold water. The giddiness left me, and I began to feel a little like a reasonable being again. My first thought was of the risk of sleeping all night in a gambling-house; my second, of the still greater risk of trying to get out after the house was closed, and of going home alone at night, through the streets of Paris with a large sum of money about me. I had slept in worse places than this on my travels, so I determined to lock, bolt, and barricade my door, and take my chance till the next morning.

Accordingly, I secured myself against all intrusion; looked under the bed, and into the cupboard; tried the fastening of the window; and then, satisfied that I had taken every proper precaution, pulled off my upper clothing, put my light, which was a dim one, on the hearth among a feathery Utter of wood ashes, and got into bed, with the handkerchief full of money under my pillow.

I soon felt not only that I could not go to sleep, but that I could not even close my eyes. I was wide awake, and in a high fever. Every nerve in my body trembled—every one of my senses seemed to be preternaturally sharpened. I tossed and rolled, and tried every kind of position, and perseveringly sought out the cold corners of the bed, and all to no purpose. Now, I thrust my arms over the clothes; now, I poked them under the clothes; now, I violently shot my legs straight out down to the bottom of the bed; now, I convulsively coiled them up as near my chin as they would go; now, I shook out my crumpled pillow, changed it to the cool side, patted it flat, and lay down quietly on my back; now, I fiercely doubled it in two, set it up on end, thrust it against the board of the bed, and tried a sitting-posture. Every effort was in vain; I groaned with vexation, as I felt that I was in for a sleepless night.

What could I do? I had no book to read. And yet, unless I found out some method of diverting my mind, I felt certain that I was in the condition to imagine all sorts of horrors; to rack my brain with forebodings of every possible and impossible danger; in short, to pass the night in suffering all conceivable varieties of nervous terror.

I raised myself on my elbow, and looked about the room—which was brightened by a lovely moonlight pouring straight through the window—to see if it contained any pictures or ornaments that I could at all clearly distinguish. While my eyes wandered from wall to wall, a remembrance of Le Maistre's delightful little book, "Voyage autour de ma Chambre," occurred to me. I resolved to imitate the French author, and find occupation and amusement enough to relieve the tedium of my wakefulness, by making a mental inventory of every article of furniture I could see, and by following up to their sources the multitude of associations which even a chair, a table, or a wash-hand stand may be made to call forth.

In the nervous unsettled state of my mind at that moment, I found it much easier to make my inventory than to make my reflections, and thereupon soon gave up all hope of thinking in Le Maistre's fanciful track—or, indeed, of thinking at all. I looked about the room at the different articles of furniture, and did nothing more.

There was, first, the bed I was lying in; a four-post bed, of all things in the world to meet with in Paris!—yes, a thorough clumsy British four-poster, with the regular top lined with chintz—the regular fringed valance all round—the regular stifling unwhole-some curtains, which I remembered having mechanically drawn back against the posts without particularly noticing the bed when I first got into the room. Then there was the marble-topped wash-hand stand, from which the water I had spilt, in my hurry to pour it out, was still dripping, slowly and more slowly, on to the brick-floor. Then two small chairs, with my coat, waistcoat, and trousers flung on them. Then a large elbow-chair covered with dirty-white dimity, with my cravat and shirt-collar thrown over the back. Then a chest of drawers with two of the brass handles off, and a tawdry, broken china inkstand placed on it by way of ornament for the top. Then the dressing-table, adorned by a very small looking-glass, and a very large pin-cushion. Then the window—an unusually large window. Then a dark old picture, which the feeble candle dimly showed me. It was the picture of a fellow in a high Spanish hat, crowned with a plume of towering feathers. A swarthy sinister ruffian, looking upward, shading his eyes with his hand, and looking intently upward—it might be at some tall gallows at which he was going to be hanged. At any rate, he had the appearance of thoroughly deserving it.

This picture put a kind of constraint upon me to look upward too—at the top of the bed. It was a gloomy and not an interesting object, and I looked back at the picture. I counted the feathers in the man's hat—they stood out in relief—three white, two green. I observed the crown of his hat, which was of a conical shape, according to the fashion supposed to have been favoured by Guido Fawkes. I wondered what he was looking up at. It couldn't be at the stars; such a desperado was neither astrologer nor astronomer. It must be at the high gallows, and he was going to be hanged presently. Would the executioner come into possession of his conical crowned hat and plume of feathers? I counted the feathers again—three white, two green.

While I still lingered over this very improving and intellectual employment, my thoughts insensibly began to wander. The moonlight shining into the room reminded me of a certain moonlight night in England—the night after a picnic party in a Welsh valley. Every incident of the drive homeward, through lovely scenery, which the moonlight made lovelier than ever, came back to my remembrance, though I had never given the picnic a thought for years; though, if I had *tried* to recollect it, I could certainly have recalled little or nothing of that scene long past. Of all the wonderful faculties that help to tell us we are immortal, which speaks the sublime truth more eloquently than memory?

Here was I, in a strange house of the most suspicious character, in a situation of uncertainty, and even of peril, which might seem to make the cool exercise of my recollection almost out of the question; nevertheless, remembering, quite involuntarily, places, people, conversations, minute circumstances of every kind, which I had thought forgotten forever, which I could not possibly have recalled at will even under the most favourable auspices. And what cause had produced in a moment the whole of this strange, complicated, mysterious effect? Nothing but some rays of moon-light shining in at my bedroom window.

I was still thinking of the picnic—of our merriment on the drive home—of the sentimental young lady who *would* quote Childe Harold because it was moonlight. I was absorbed by these past scenes and past amusements, when, in an instant, the thread on which my memories hung snapped asunder: my attention immediately came back to present things more vividly than ever, and I found myself, I neither knew why nor wherefore, looking hard at the picture again.

Looking for what?

Good God, the man had pulled his hat down on his brows!—No! the hat itself was gone! Where was the conical crown? Where the feathers—three white, two green? Not there! In place of the hat and feathers, what dusky object was it that now hid his forehead, his eyes, his shading hand?

Was the bed moving?

I turned on my back and looked up. Was I mad? drunk? dreaming? giddy again? or was the top of the bed really moving down—sinking slowly, regularly, silently, horribly, right down throughout the whole of its length and breadth—right down upon Me, as I lay underneath?

My blood seemed to stand still. A deadly paralyzing coldness stole all over me, as I turned my head round on the pillow, and determined to test whether the bed-top was really moving or not, by keeping my eye on the man in the picture.

The next look in that direction was enough. The dull, black, frowsy outline of the valance above me was within an inch of being parallel with his waist. I still looked breathlessly. And steadily, and slowly—very slowly—I saw the figure, and the line of frame below the figure, vanish, as the valance moved down before it.

I am, constitutionally, anything but timid. I have been on more than one occasion in peril of my life, and have not lost my self-possession for an instant; but when the conviction first settled on my mind that the bed-top was really moving, was steadily and continuously sinking down upon me, I looked up shuddering, helpless, panic-stricken, beneath the hideous machinery for murder, which was advancing closer and closer to suffocate me where I lay.

I looked up, motionless, speechless, breathless. The candle, fully spent, went out; but the moonlight still brightened the room. Down and down, without pausing and without sounding, came the bed-top, and still my panic-terror seemed to bind me faster and faster to the mattress on which I lay—down and down it sank, till the dusty odour from the lining of the canopy came stealing into my nostrils.

At that final moment the instinct of self-preservation startled me out of my trance, and I moved at last. There was just room for me to roll myself sideways off the bed. As I dropped noiselessly to the floor, the edge of the murderous canopy touched me on the shoulder.

Without stopping to draw my breath, without wiping the cold sweat from my face, I rose instantly on my knees to watch the bed-top. I was literally spell-bound by it. If I had heard footsteps behind me, I could not have turned round; if a means of escape had been miraculously provided for me, I could not have moved to take advantage of it. The whole life in me was, at that moment, concentrated in my eyes.

It descended—the whole canopy, with the fringe round it, came down—down—close down; so close that there was not room now to squeeze my finger between the bed-top and the bed. I felt at the sides, and discovered that what had appeared to me from beneath to be the ordinary light canopy of a four post bed, was in reality a thick, broad mattress, the substance of which was concealed by the valance and its fringe. I looked up and saw the four posts rising hideously bare. In the middle of the bed-top was a huge wooden screw that had evidently worked it down through a hole in the ceiling, just as ordinary presses are worked down on the substance selected for compression. The frightful apparatus moved without making the faintest noise. There had been no creaking as it came down; there was now not the faintest sound from the room above. Amid a dead and awful silence I beheld before me—in the nineteenth century, and in the civilized capital of France—such a machine for secret murder by suffocation as might have existed in the worst days of the Inquisition, in the lonely inns among the Hartz Mountains, in the mysterious tribunals of Westphalia! Still, as I looked on it, I could not move, I could hardly breathe, but I began to recover the power of thinking, and in a moment I discovered the murderous conspiracy framed against me in all its horror.

My cup of coffee had been drugged, and drugged too strongly. I had been saved from being smothered by having taken an overdose of some narcotic. How I had chafed and fretted at the fever-fit which had preserved my life by keeping me awake! How recklessly I had confided myself to the two wretches who had led me into this room, determined, for the sake of my winnings, to kill me in my sleep by the surest and most horrible contrivance for secretly accomplishing my destruction! How many men, winners like me, had slept, as I had proposed to sleep, in that bed, and had never been seen or heard of more! I shuddered at the bare idea of it.

But, erelong, all thought was again suspended by the sight of the murderous canopy moving once more. After it had remained on the bed—as nearly as I could guess—about ten minutes, it began to move up again. The villains who worked it from above evidently believed that their purpose was now accomplished. Slowly and silently, as it had descended, that horrible bed-top rose towards its former place. When it reached the upper extremities of the four posts, it reached the ceiling too. Neither hole nor screw could be seen; the bed became in appearance an ordinary bed again—the canopy an ordinary canopy, even to the most suspicious eyes.

Now, for the first time, I was able to move—to rise from my knees—to dress myself in my upper clothing—and to consider of how I should escape. If I betrayed, by the smallest noise, that the attempt to suffocate me had failed, I was certain to be murdered. Had I made any noise already? I listened intently, looking towards the door.

No! no footsteps in the passage outside—no sound of a tread, light or heavy, in the room above—absolute silence everywhere. Besides locking and bolting my door, I had moved an old wooden chest against it, which I had found under the bed. To remove this chest (my blood ran cold as I thought what its contents *might* be!) without making some disturbance was impossible; and, moreover, to think of escaping through the house, now barred up for the night, was sheer insanity. Only one chance was left me—the window. I stole to it on tiptoe.

My bedroom was on the first floor, above an *entresol,* and looked into the back street, which you have sketched in your view. I raised my hand to open the window, knowing that on that action hung, by the merest hair's breadth, my chance of safety. They keep vigilant watch in a House of Murder. If any part of the frame cracked, if the hinge creaked, I was a lost man ! It must have occupied me at least five minutes, reckoning by time—five *hours,* reckoning by suspense—to open that window. I succeeded in doing it silently—in doing it with all the dexterity of a housebreaker—and then looked down into the street. To leap the distance beneath me would be almost certain destruction! Next, I looked round at the sides of the house. Down the left side ran the thick water-pipe which you have drawn—it passed close by the outer edge of the window. The moment I saw the pipe, I knew I was saved. My breath came and went freely for the first time since I had seen the canopy of the bed moving down upon me!

To some men the means of escape which I had discovered might have seemed difficult and dangerous enough—to *me* the prospect of slipping down the pipe into the street did not suggest even a thought of peril. I had always been accustomed, by the practice of gymnastics, to keep up my schoolboy powers as a daring and expert climber; and knew that my head, hands, and feet would serve me faithfully in any hazards of ascent or descent. I had already got one leg over the window-sill, when I remembered the handkerchief filled with money under my pillow. I could well have afforded to leave it behind me, but I was revengefully determined that the miscreants of the gambling-house should miss their plunder as well as their victim. So I went back to the bed and tied the heavy handkerchief at my back by my cravat.

Just as I had made it tight and fixed it in a comfortable place, I thought I heard a sound of breathing outside the door. The chill feeling of horror ran through me again as I listened. No! dead silence still in the passage—I had only heard the night-air blowing softly into the room. The next moment I was on the window sill—and the next I had a firm grip on the water-pipe with my hands and knees.

I slid down into the street easily and quietly, as I thought I should, and immediately set off at the top of my speed to a branch 'Prefecture' of Police, which I knew was situated in the immediate neighbourhood. A 'Sub-prefect,' and several picked men among his subordinates, happened to be up, maturing, I believe, some scheme for discovering the perpetrator of a mysterious murder which all Paris was talking of just then. When I began my story, in a breathless hurry and in very bad French, I could see that the Sub-prefect suspected me of being a drunken Englishman who had robbed somebody; but he soon altered his opinion as I went on, and before I had anything like concluded, he shoved all the papers before him into a drawer, put on his hat, supplied me with another (fori was bare-headed), ordered a file of soldiers, desired his expert followers to get ready all sorts of tools for breaking open doors and ripping up brick-flooring, and took my arm, in the most friendly and familiar manner possible, to lead me with him out of the house. I will venture to say, that when the Sub-prefect was a little boy, and was taken for the first time to the Play, he was not half as much pleased as he was now at the job in

WILKIE COLLINS 111

prospect for him at the gambling-house !

Away we went through the streets, the Sub-prefect cross-examining and congratulating me in the same breath as we marched at the head of our formidable *posse comitatus.* Sentinels were placed at the back and front of the house the moment we got to it; a tremendous battery of knocks was directed against the door; a light appeared at a window; I was told to conceal myself behind the police—then came more knocks, and a cry of "Open in the name of the law!" At that terrible summons bolts and locks gave way before an invisible hand, and the moment after the Sub-prefect was in the passage, confronting a waiter half-dressed and ghastly pale. This was the short dialogue which immediately took place—

"We want to see the Englishman who is sleeping in this house."

"He went away hours ago."

"He did no such thing. His friend went away; *he* remained. Show us to his bedroom!"

"I swear to you, Monsieur le Sous-prefet, he is not here! He—"

"I swear to you, Monsieur le Garcon, he is. He slept here—he didn't find your bed comfortable—he came to us to complain of it—here he is among my men—and here am I ready to look for a flea or two in his bedstead. Renaudin! (calling to one of the subordinates, and pointing to the waiter) collar that man, and tie his hands behind him. Now, then, gentlemen, let us walk up stairs!"

Every man and woman in the house was secured—the 'Old Soldier' the first. Then I identified the bed in which I had slept, and then we went into the room above.

No object that was at all extraordinary appeared in any part of it. The Sub-prefect looked round the place, commanded everybody to be silent, stamped twice on the floor, called for a candle, looked attentively at the spot he had stamped on, and ordered the flooring there to be carefully taken up. This was done in no time. Lights were produced, and we saw a deep raftered cavity between the floor of this room and the ceiling of the room beneath.

Through this cavity there ran perpendicularly a sort of case of iron thickly greased; and inside the case appeared the screw, which communicated with the bed-top below. Extra lengths of screw, freshly oiled; levers covered with felt; all the complete upper works of a heavy press—constructed with infernal ingenuity so as to join the fixtures below, and when taken to pieces again to go into the smallest possible compass—were next discovered and pulled out on the floor. After some little difficulty the Sub-prefect succeeded in putting the machinery together, and, leaving his men to work it, descended with me to the bedroom. The smothering canopy was then lowered, but not so noiselessly as I had seen it lowered. When I mentioned this to the Sub-prefect, his answer, simple as it was. had a terrible significance.

"My men," said he, "are working down the bed-top for the first time—the men whose money you won were in better practice."

We left the house in the sole possession of two police agents—everyone of the inmates being removed to prison on the spot. The Sub-prefect, after taking down my *"proces-verbal"* in his office, returned with me to my hotel to get my passport. "Do you think," I asked, as I gave it to him, "that any men have really been smothered in that bed, as they tried to smother *me?*"

"I have seen dozens of drowned men laid out at the Morgue," answered the Sub-prefect, "in whose pocket-books were found letters, stating that they had committed suicide in the Seine, because they had lost everything at the gaming-table. Do I know how many of those men entered the same gambling-house that you entered? won as *you* won? took that bed as *you* took it? slept in it? were smothered in it? and were privately thrown into the river, with a letter of explanation written by the murderers and placed in their pocket-books? No man can say how many or how few have suffered the fate from which you have escaped. The people of the gambling-house kept their bedstead machinery a secret from us—even from the police! The dead kept the rest of the secret for them. Good night, or rather good morning, Monsieur Faulkner! Be at my office again at nine o'clock—in the meantime, *au revoir!*"

The rest of my story is soon told. I was examined and reexamined; the gambling-house was strictly searched all through from top to bottom; the prisoners were separately interrogated; and two of the less guilty among them made a confession. I discovered that the Old Soldier was the master of the gambling house—*justice* discovered that he had been drummed out of the army as a vagabond years ago; that he had been guilty of all sorts of villanies since; that he was in possession of stolen property, which the owners identified; and that he, the croupier, another accomplice, and the woman who had made my cup of coffee, were all in the secret of the bedstead. Here appeared some reason to doubt whether the inferior persons attached to the house knew anything of the suffocating machinery; and they received the benefit of that doubt, by being treated simply as thieves and vagabonds. As for the Old Soldier and his two head myrmidons, they went to the galleys; the woman who had drugged my coffee was imprisoned for I forget how many years; the regular attendants at the gambling-house were considered 'suspicious,' and placed under 'surveillance;' and I became, for one whole week (which is a long time), the head 'lion' in Parisian society. My adventure was dramatised by three illustrious playmakers, but never saw theatrical daylight; for the censorship forbade the introduction on the stage of a correct copy of the gambling-house bedstead.

One good result was produced by my adventure which any censorship must have approved—it cured me of ever again trying *"Rouge et Noir"* as an amusement. The sight of a green cloth, with packs of cards and heaps of money on it, will henceforth be forever associated in my mind with the sight of a bed canopy descending to suffocate me in the silence and darkness of the night.

TEA WITH EMMA WHITEHALL

AND ANDREW McCURDY

Emma, I just wanted to begin by thanking you for agreeing to do this interview. The general consensus during our Gallery readthroughs was that The Rat and the Frog was a fun story. I personally felt the central character was well-imagined in both her role as the maid and her alter ego, the Rat Prince. What was the genesis of Ida and did she evolve as a character during your writing?

Emma:

You know, I can't really remember Ida's genesis. More likely than not, she came about during a session at my writing group. With her character, I really wanted to play with the different facets of her personality—she's always a quiet, fairly dry person, but there's a sarcasm and a wit in the Rat Prince that would be classed as very unseemly in Ida the maid. And there's another side to her, I think, that does long for connection—a side Ida won't ever really admit, even to herself.

Andrew:
Though the story is relatively short, you did a nice job fleshing out some of the central character's motif, modus operandi, and even introduced some minor characters. Are there more Rat Prince stories in the works?

Emma:
Ida is actually part of a much, much wider world. For the last year and a half, I've been working on a collection of short stories set in the Steampunk city where she lives - it's finally done, and looking for a new home with a publisher. I wanted to create a world where the lives of the characters intertwine and overlap. Doctor Odessa Malko (the scientist who captured the Hippocamps at the museum) has her own story, as do a multitude of other characters that you haven't met yet...

Andrew:
What do you like most about steampunk, and what do you like most about your steampunk city?

Emma:
I feel like Steampunk is such a flexible genre - it's a place where science fiction and fantasy can blend together somewhat. I've found it creates a space where, as a writer, you can really play. My favourite thing about my city is that there are so many characters hiding in it! Just last week, someone new sauntered up to one of my main characters, and began flirting with them. I've spent most of my writing time since trying to make them see sense, but it seems to be falling on deaf ears...

Andrew:
What is your favourite line from your own writing (published or not) and what was the context behind it?

Emma:
"And so, over the next twelve minutes, Ida Finn silently descended into the depths of her own personal hell" really made me laugh when I wrote it. Because I've been writing these characters for so long now, I've really got to know them - and I know how much watching her employer and her beau in an

intimate situation would horrify Ida. Eldritch beings don't faze the Rat Prince, but Devon Casterbury has the potential to send her spiralling into madness.

Andrew:
What distracts you most from writing and finishing a story?

Emma:
I always have to write in the mornings, because by the time I come in from work, all I want to do is watch Netflix, eat junk food, and rest. That's partially why "The Rat and the Frog" was written at my writing group: it's two hours where I am expected to write, and I have to have something to read to the group at the end!

Andrew:
What is your process for editing your work once you have finished a draft?

Emma:
A lot of my edits happen either as I'm writing the story (usually technical edits, like punctuation or word choices), or days/weeks later, when I'm thinking over what happens, how this character interacts with this one, or *this* might be an interesting piece of character development, etc. My partner and my writing friends are also great editing tools, as I need to make sure the story is perfect before they get to read it!

Andrew:
Who are some of your favourite authors

*from the past and who are you currently reading? As a follow-up,
what do you ook l for when you read the works of other authors?*

Emma:
I've just started reading "The Cabin at the End of the World" by
Paul Tremblay - it's very intense! In general, I love fantasy and
horror writers who do something different with their genre, and
who use otherworldly tropes as a tool to explore our deepest
thoughts and emotions - John Adjvide Lindqvist is a favourite of
mine, as is Joe Hill. Fiction about mermaids seems to be very on-
trend right now in the UK, and it all seems to fall into a
historical/super-natural place that I'm really enjoying - "The
Mermaid and Mrs. Hancock" and Christina Henry's "The
Mermaid" are both brilliant reads, if you enjoyed "The Rat and
the Frog".

Andrew:
*What do value the most in feedback and reviews from your
readers?*

Emma:
I want to know if my characters have made an impact on you. The
minutia of the world - how exactly do Ida's goggles work, how was
the frog-thing captured in the first place - don't matter to me, as
long as Ida, Lucinda, and even Devon Casterbury read like real
human beings.

*What do you like best about being a writer, and conversely, what
frustrates you the most about being a writer?*

Emma:
I wish I had a tube that connected my brain to my computer, so I
didn't have to go to the trouble of typing my stories up -
sometimes I wish they just appeared, fully formed, as they are in
my head! But I love watching ideas and stories form in my head as
I'm writing, or even just daydreaming on the bus to work. They
come from somewhere in the mist of my brain, take shape, and
then go into your head, and take on a new form in there! I think
that's amazing.

CUSTOMER SERVICE
OF THE PRIESTHOOD OF THIKRA, DESTROYER OF WORLDS AND CREATOR OF LIGHT
YASMINE FAHMY

Hello. You have reached the Priesthood of Thikra, Destroyer of Worlds and Creator of Light. Your devotion is very important to us.

To continue in Thikran chanting, most pleasing to the goddess, press 1. For unholy netherworldly shrieking, press 2. For inferior mortal English, press 3.

You have chosen to continue in: inferior mortal English. The cost of this call is 0.07 prayers per minute. Please note that this call is being recorded, as Thikra is all-seeing, all-knowing.

To inquire after your balance, press 1. To—

You have: 258 prayer points and: 64 hours of good service.

Please note that patience is a virtue. Pressing a button before hearing all the options is impatient. 1 prayer point has been deducted from your balance. You now have: 257 prayer points and: 64 hours of good service.

To contest this deduction, please press 1. To request–

You have chosen to contest the will of the Goddess. You doubt her words. This does not fall within the tenets of absolute surrender that she requires. 50 prayer points have been deducted from your balance. You now have: 207 prayer points and: 64 hours of good service.

To show your contrition, you will remain silent for: 2 minutes.

Please enjoy this selection of hymns from three centuries ago praising the Divine Thikra.

Thank you for your obedience. Do note that any attempted deception by leaving the phone and not listening patiently to the hymns praising the Divine Thikra will have been noted by Thikra and her all-seeing eye. In her mercy, she has chosen to forgive. No further deductions will be made.

For an individual service, press 1. For group services, press 2. If the intended recipient of the individual service is not you, press 1. If it is you, press 2. Please note that if you are possessed by at least one ancient spirit, whether saintly or malevolent, you do not qualify for an individual service. If you would like to return to the previous menu because you miscounted, press 0.

To bask in the glory of Thikra, press 1. To lodge a complaint against a fellow man, press 2. To confess to your crimes against the Goddess, press 3, despite the fact she already knows for she is all-knowing. To redeem your points for rewards, press 4.

Incorrect. You must always bask in the glory of Thikra. For this transgression 10 prayer points have been deducted from your balance. You now have: 197 prayer points and 60 hours of good service.

To bask in the glory of Thikra, press 1.

To meditate on the wisdom of Thikra, Destroyer of Worlds and Creator of Light, press 1. To sing the Goddess' praises, press 2. To provide a list of things for which you are thankful, press 3. To donate in the Goddess' name, press 4. To offer sacrifices, press 5.

You now have: 2 minutes, in which to list things the Goddess has provided for which you are thankful.

Sorry. We could not understand your gratitude. Please try again. Be sure to speak in a clear loud voice and invoke all 23 of the Goddess' names beforehand, as is customary.

Your basking has been accepted. Thank you for your devotion.

To lodge a complaint against a fellow man, press 2. To confess to your crimes against the Goddess, press 3, despite the fact she already knows for she is all-knowing. To redeem your points for rewards, press 4. For other services, press 5.

For blessings, press 1. For divine revelations, press 2. For small miracles, press 3. For large miracles, press 4, and hope the Goddess is feeling generous. For a petition to change the course of your predestined life, press 5. To donate prayer points to a temple of your choice, press 6. To convert good service hours into prayer points, press 7. To convert prayer points into good service hours, press 8.

To submit a new petition, press 1. To inquire after the status of an existing petition, press 2.

Incorrect. You must have: 1 small miracle in order for the goddess to accept your petition to change the course of your predestined life.

For blessings, press 1. For divine revelations, press 2. For small miracles, press 3. For large miracles, press 4, and hope the Goddess is feeling generous. For a petition to change the course of your predestined life, press 5. To donate prayer points to a temple of your choice, press 6. To convert good service hours into prayer points, press 7. To convert prayer points into good service hours, press 8.

The cost of a small miracle is: 150 prayer points. This cost is non-refundable.

For miracles over nature, press 1. For miracles of healing, press 2. For miracles to keep your wife from leaving you and running away with your coworker, press 3. For miracles to actively harm your coworker and thus render him unable to run *anywhere,* press 4.

You have chosen to wish harm upon another human. This is a sin. Only the Goddess Thikra may decide to dole out punishment.

Your balance is now: 47 prayer points and 60 hours of good service.

Repent and press 0 to return to the previous menu.

To lodge a complaint against a fellow man, press 2. To confess to your crimes against the Goddess, press 3, despite the fact she already knows for she is All Knowing. To redeem your points for rewards, press—

Curse words are unacceptable. 2 prayer points have been de—

Patience is a virtue. 1 prayer point has been—

1 prayer point has been deducted. Your balance is now—

Thank you for calling. Your transgressions have been noted.

CONTRIBUTORS

Donald J. Bingle is the author of six books and more than fifty shorter works in the horror, thriller, science fiction, fantasy, steampunk, mystery, romance, comedy, and memoir genres. *The Love-Haight Case Files,* his mystery/horror/romance/urban fantasy novel (with Jean Rabe), won three Silver Falchions. More at www.donaldjbingle.com.

Wilkie Collins (1824-1889) was an English novelist, playwright, and short story writer. He began his career as a clerk to a tea merchant and later became a close friend and collaborator to Charles Dickens. He attributed his early skill in storytelling to a boarding school bully who would not allow him to go to sleep until he had told him a story.

Yasmine Fahmy lives in Cairo, Egypt, where she spends her time hiding from the sun, her students, and the djinn to whom she sold her soul for inspiration. It never delivered on the inspiration front, you see. Her work has appeared in *Daily Science Fiction* and *The Sockdolager.*

Grace P. Fong ("Fictograph") is a Vancouver-based illustrator for speculative fiction, specializing in personal and promotional work for authors. In 2018, she was nominated for a Hugo award for Best Fan Artist for her work with Alyssa Wong and *Uncanny Magazine.* She also likes to write, travel, eat, and annoy her cat.

Julie Frost lives in Utah with her family—six guinea pigs, three humans, a tripod calico cat, and a kitten who thinks she's a warrior princess. Her short fiction has appeared in many venues, and her novel, *Pack Dynamics,* was published by WordFire Press in 2015. She whines about writing, a lot, at agilebrit.livejournal.com

William Burton McCormick is a Nevada native and Hawthornden Castle Fellowship winner. He has lived ten years in Ukraine and visited Odessa, the setting of "Kutsenko's Cage" numerous times. The story's protagonists, sisters Tasia and Eleni Karadopoulina, debuted in the Derringer Award-nominated story "The Antiquary's Wife" in *Alfred Hitchcock's Mystery Magazine*, March 2013.

Andrew McCurdy is a writer and editor whose day job as a Speech-Language Pathologist involves helping nonverbal, special needs children access technology to maximize their ability to communicate. He lives in rural Nova Scotia with a ten-year-old girl and two cats. In between short stories, he has been diligently working on his masterpiece novel for what feels like the past ninety-two years. He credits Charleton Heston's angst while kneeling in the surf, cursing the half-buried Statue of Liberty, as the genesis for his love of science fiction.

Born far too late to meet Jules Verne, **Steven R. Southard** pays homage to the Father of Science Fiction in his steampunk stories. Explore Steve's website at stevenrsouthard.com to share the wonder and adventure of his intriguing characters and their amazing machines.

Justin Tiang is a Singapore-based concept artist and illustrator for games, television, and film. Justin is pledged to Wonder, which he is able to find just about everywhere. He sings, wanders, and rears bugs for hobbies. View more of his work at tiangpong.com and 28crucis.deviantart.com

Marcelina Vizcarra has moved over thirty times, most recently to Tennessee where she explores the woods and waterways with her kids, partner in crime, and their dog. Her writing has appeared or is forthcoming in *Nature Futures, Flash Fiction Online, Timeshift*, and other speculative and literary publications.

Emma Whitehall is a writer, editor and book reviewer from the North East of England. Her work has been published in the UK, USA, Mexico and Ireland, and was shortlisted for the 2017 Fish Flash Fiction Award. You can follow her at @Hire_Emma.

This issue of CURIOSITIES was made by

Kevin Frost - Lead Editor, Typesetting
Andrew McCurdy - Editor, Interviewer
Jed Dagger - First Reader
Steadman Kondor - First Reader
Kris Law - Majordomo
　　　　　to Mr. Underby

And with help from our
　Splendid Patrons

　　Mimielle
　Bookworm
　& Scott

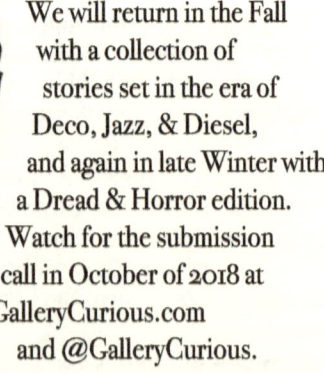

We will return in the Fall
with a collection of
stories set in the era of
Deco, Jazz, & Diesel,
and again in late Winter with
a Dread & Horror edition.
Watch for the submission
call in October of 2018 at
GalleryCurious.com
and @GalleryCurious.

This volume was set in Bodoni 72 after the serif
typefaces designed by Giambattista Bodoni
in the late 18th Century, which were considered modern until some time in
the 20th Century. Agga Swist-
blnk of Indonesia drew the
interior display font
which is called
Banthers.